THE MODERN BREAK-UP

DANIEL CHIDIAC

UNDERCOVER
PUBLISHING HOUSE

The Modern Break-Up

Copyright © 2019 by Daniel Chidiac. All rights reserved.

First published by Undercover Publishing House.

ISBN: 978-0-9871665-5-5

This book is dedicated to life.
–Daniel Chidiac

The Modern Break-Up

ENDLESS KNOT

Her eyes opened slowly and then closed again. She hadn't yet processed that she was in a place that was unfamiliar to her. But as she took another glimpse, fear suddenly took over her like a child being locked in a dark room. Her body froze; her mind raced.

Lying on a dirt path a few feet wide and only wearing a white dress, she was cold and alone. There were two high walls on either side of her that went as far as she could see. They were made of thick, dry branches. Nothing was visible through them. They blocked her in. The sky was gray, dulling everything beneath it. There was no life here, no sound, no color. She quickly stood up and walked around in a daze. *Where am I?*

Frantically trying to find a way out, she tried escaping through the walls. With every failed attempt, the sharp branches cut her. She ran and ran and ran as fast as she could. As she got to the end of the path, she noticed similar paths to her left and right. She turned left. Getting to the end of that path, something dawned on her...she had been here before. She was in the maze.

It wasn't exactly how she remembered it. Once luscious and full of life, people would hold hands and laugh. Now it was abandoned, silent. She tried to remember how she got out last time, but her memory failed her.

"Help! Help! Someone, please help me!" she yelled in desperation and fell to her knees. Scared for her life, not knowing what her future held, she sobbed uncontrollably. Her tears splashed on the ground, giving it the only bit of moisture it had had in months. After a few minutes, the sun's rays started to warm her face. There wasn't much cracking through the dense clouds, but it was enough to give her hope. She had to get up . . .

As she wiped her cheeks dry and composed herself, she saw what seemed to be a light at the end of yet another path. She sprinted toward it. To her, that light seemed like the only option. Getting closer, a figure started to appear. It was radiating. She finally arrived and saw who it was.

"Oh, thank God. I knew you'd come to save me. I've been scared for my life. What the hell are we doing here? Where have you been?"

He didn't answer, just smiled, as his hands remained behind his back.

"What are you holding?" she asked.

Again, he didn't answer. Looking innocently into her eyes, he revealed what he'd been hiding and gifted her a bunch of bright red roses. It was the only real color she had seen so far.

"Thank you," she said, accepting his gift. She closed her eyes and relished in the soft petals as they rubbed lightly against the tip of her nose. The scent was so beautiful, so fresh that for a moment she forgot where she was.

With her eyes still closed, she heard a quiet hiss. A snake slithered up from within the roses.

Just as she went to drop them, it sprung up and bit her, the fangs clenching firmly on her lips.

Screaming in shock, she pulled it off with all her strength and threw it to the ground. She frantically screamed at him, "Why? Why?" and began beating on his chest. With every hit, a hollow sound rang out and his radiance left. Eventually, stiff, lifeless, like an empty statue, he fell over.

She ran for her life. With every stride, she could feel the pain of the dry path on the soles of her bare feet. Still running as fast she could, she looked back to see if danger was following her. Not seeing where she was running, she smashed into something and fell to the ground. Everything went blank. A few minutes passed.

She slowly stood up and noticed that it was a gigantic mirror as wide as the path that had stopped her in her tracks. There was no getting past it. She had to face it. She just stared at herself, and what she saw consumed every part of her being. The bite from the gift had deformed her face.

"You're so ugly compared to them. Look at you. No wonder he doesn't want you!" she yelled at herself in the mirror. As she continued, a quote appeared on the glass:

Sometimes, where pure light is perceived, darkness lingers.

Not being able to ease the voices in her head, she gave in to rage. She smashed the mirror with her fist; blood poured down from her knuckles. Looking to the sky, she let out one last cry and fell into the darkness of her mind.

CHAPTER 1

THAT GUY

"He's so hot," Zara said as she took a sip of her espresso martini.

"Who?" I asked.

"The one near the bar with the white shirt on. But don't look yet. I don't want to make it obvious. In a minute, just pretend you're looking around and have a quick look."

"Don't be so stupid. I'm looking now," I said.

Zara quickly grabbed my arm. "Can you not!"

I tried not to get under her skin, so I ridiculously looked around the bar in an effort to disguise my curiosity.

"I think I just saw him. There were three guys with white on. Which one?" I asked.

Zara moved into a different position for me to have another subtle look. "Are you serious? One's fat, the other looks like his face has been hit with a baseball bat. The gorgeous one, Amelia, obviously," she said in her judgmental but honest tone.

"Okay, calm down."

"Well?"

"Yeah, he's beautiful. He looks European or something," I said.

All I could see was a guy who looked like he didn't care whether he would ever speak to me or not. Just by the way he was leaning on the bar, he looked confident enough to make me feel insecure. But rather than deterring me, it made me even more curious. I almost had this feeling like I had to try to equal his energy, and the only way I could do that was by not giving him the attention he probably always got. I needed to play it cool.

Weird things happen to me when I'm faced with a guy I'm really attracted to. I feel like I have to prove that I'm not desperate. I'll control how many times I text him and analyze my actions. Usually it's not really anything they do that makes my behavior change; it's me. I get nervous. I almost always do something that makes me look like a psycho. And sometimes, because I know I'm going to screw it up, I stop communication before I can. They probably think I avoid them because I'm not interested, but sometimes it's because I'm so intimidated that being myself goes out the window. In a perfect world, I would act with the guys I'm attracted to the way I do with guys I don't really care about.

There's something great about not being genuinely interested. Because then I have more power within myself. I'm not vulnerable. I can stay who I am and think clearly. When I'm too attracted, I lose all of that. I lose control. I couldn't tell you how many times I have sworn that I won't give a guy more of my attention than he deserves. But sure enough, someone comes along that makes me a hypocrite. And I always kick myself for it. Sometimes I question, if we're really interested in someone—too interested, maybe—can we act like we're not, or are we doomed as soon as our mind even plays around with the idea that they are better than I am?

From across the bar, I saw that guy smile at his friend in conversation. I nearly died ... I'm a massive sucker for a nice smile. His white sneakers, frayed light blue jeans, and slightly unbuttoned linen white shirt all just worked. I'm no fashion guru, but I know when I see a guy who knows what he's doing. There were other guys in the bar who looked nice but too put together, too pretty. Not to mention they looked like they had spent more time doing their hair than I did. This guy had scruffy, dark-blondish hair. Bed hair but hot. He just seemed to look that way with no effort. His sleeves were rolled up loosely above his wrist and his shirt hung perfectly. I snuck as many glances as I could while pretending to look back and forth at the DJ not far behind him. My mind started to race ... *I wonder if he's seen me look at him. His tan is so sexy. I think he's from overseas.*

"I love that scruffy beard look on tanned skin," Zara said as she interrupted my daydream.

I snapped back into reality. "Yeah, he has the perfect length."

Zara put her nearly finished drink on the bar. "Did you just see that?"

"What?" I replied.

"He just checked you out."

"No, he didn't."

"He did. Keep looking. See?"

"Oh my God, he did. I look like shit, though," I replied, quickly turning away and nervously touching my face.

"Smile at him," Zara said as she sucked down the last bit of her drink.

"I'm not in the mood. Not after everything that's happened the past few weeks," I said.

"I'm doing this for you. You're ready. But do what you want. I'm on this vacation to have fun," she said, going through her overpacked clutch.

"I'm ready? How long did it take you to get over that guy who was five years younger than you? You were obsessed with him and you only met him once," I said.

At times, Zara has a tendency to give advice that she doesn't follow. I know she has good intentions, but it still frustrates the hell out of me sometimes.

She looked up at me. "I told you I can't really explain why I was so hung up on him. Some just get caught in the web ... they stick around."

"What web?" I threw back.

"There's always a guy—or a few guys, actually— out of all the guys you meet who stick around in your mind for a long time. They're in 'the web.' You think about 'em from time to time or you see a post of theirs on Insta and you reach out. There's still a bit of hope they'll catch up with you again. And it goes around in a circle," she said. "When you do contact them, you wait by your phone like an idiot for them to respond. Instead you should be telling them to fuck off or ignore them if they do randomly decide to message because they want a booty call, but you don't. When they want to hang out, you'll drop everything for them. You're weaker with them than the rest. And the shit thing is, they can be caught in that web for years. They hang around because the situation didn't go the way you wanted it to. It doesn't mean you wanted to marry them—you just want them to chase your ass instead. You want the power," she continued, rustling through her clutch again.

"What are you looking for?" I replied.

She tried to ignore me, keeping her head down while mumbling under her breath, "I'm just seeing how much cash I have left."

I knew she was lying to me; I could feel it.

"Look, I know you're still down about him, and you know I understand, but we're in New York for a reason. We're both single now; we only live once. Seriously, think about it. In a few days, you're going to go back to the same routine and seeing the same people. Just let go and have some fun. You used to be the tough one out of us. You'll be fine," Zara continued passionately.

I knew it! She has coke. That little speech is Zara's way of trying to convince me to have a "good" night. If I ask her, it's going to start a whole new conversation. *Maybe I'll get tempted to do some as well.* My mind started to play around with the idea of letting go. There was a part of me that just wanted to forget Jay and have fun.

"I know what you've got."

Zara stopped rustling through her clutch and sighed. "Okay, don't give me a headache over it. I haven't touched it in more than a month. We're here for a few more nights, so let's just chill out before we have to get back into 'work mode' next week. Anyway, it's just coke. You'll be fine tomorrow. Plus, I've got CBD oil and melatonin for us to sleep later. Oh, and xannys if we really need them."

"More than a month? You called me, saying, 'I swear on my life I'm never touching that stuff again,' after your big night with Loren three weeks ago. Not to mention you just went to a spiritual Yoga retreat," I said.

"Yeah, I went to a Yoga retreat and I party sometimes. We all have our way of letting go. I don't have to be straight as an arrow to be spiritual or have self-awareness. I'm a free spirit. I live on impulse, and sometimes that causes me to act spontaneously and live on the edge. I'm not a nun and I don't pretend to be," she replied.

"Chill out, I was only joking. You know I'm not judging you," I replied, feeling bad for giving her shit about it.

I didn't know why I was acting so edgy toward Zara. I think it was just the stress this asshole has put me through the past few weeks. And to be honest, I didn't know where the night was going to end if I did coke with her. I felt like, with everything going on at the moment, I needed to stay in control of my mind. I decided against it. That stuff messes with my emotions. I know it's hard for Zara to see me like some sort of "drag along," but I just wasn't in the right frame of mind to be getting too crazy.

Zara shook her head at me. "Look at you. You're beautiful. You're smart. Others are dying of starvation around the world, and we're worried about bullshit. We don't have anyone to answer to. How many people just get to pack up and come to New York when they feel like it? Huh? Do you know how many married women I know who wish they could do this?" she said, trying everything she had to convince me.

"Nah, babe, I'd better not. Honestly, I don't care if you do it, but I'll just stick with alcohol. I'm having a good time, don't worry. I'm going to get another vodka. You want an espresso martini?" I answered.

"Yes, please. And tell them to make it stronger this time. Oh, what the fuck does he want now?" Zara said while looking at her phone.

"Who?" I replied.

"That guy I told you I met at Loren's birthday. Seriously, he's so annoying. I'm trying to be nice and let him down gently because we have mutual friends, but he won't take the hint. I'm on the verge of saying something really mean," she said.

"Maybe he really likes you."

"He doesn't even know me. And I don't care. I don't like him. I can't help my feelings. For the past month, I have used the same excuse not to catch up. I keep telling him my friend is going through a breakup and I need to be with her. The thing is, he just found out about your breakup through Loren. Now he thinks it's the real reason I'm not catching up. Shit…I should have said something else—"

"What? Is that bitch telling everyone about my breakup?" I interrupted.

"Don't worry. It probably came up in conversation innocently. Anyway, he just texted me saying, 'Hey babe, how are you? I heard about Amelia, so all good for now. I thought you were just saying that to avoid me. Haha. I'll contact you soon to see how everything is. Smiley face,'" Zara read to me, cringing.

"At least you're wanted," I half-joked. "What happened to that girl? The singer from Bumble?" I replied.

"Oh yeah ... I wanted to meet her, but she seems boring," she said.

"How? You haven't even met her."

"Well, the first message she ever sent me was, 'Hey, how are you?' No emotion, nothing. Then after that, she's just blunt in her texts. Sometimes she puts smiley faces but the old school ones. Never emojis or anything."

"You're actually joking, right?" I said in disgust.

"No. Why?"

"Zara! How can you judge someone so quickly? I thought you were deeper than that," I said.

Zara doesn't discriminate in her attraction toward both sexes and in her judgment toward them at times too. She's straight down the middle.

"I want to get to know someone before I meet up with them," she answered.

"How are you going to get to know someone if you don't ever meet them? That's part of the reason things are fucked these days, the reason we don't understand each other. We don't even have the respect to look someone in the eye and speak to them. We're so quick to assume or judge on the most pathetic things," I said.

"Yeah okay, fair enough. But what if I get bored five minutes into the date?" she said, having a sip of her drink.

"And what if you don't? What happened to giving people a real chance?" I asked. "Remember Jake? The guy I was sort of seeing before Jay?"

"Yeah. I loved Jake," Zara answered.

"Yeah, and you always said how much fun he was. What you don't know is that he was literally the most boring texter. When I met him, I had one of the best dates I've ever had. And after getting to know him, I realized he took longer to open up. And other guys I thought I'd connected with over text were a disaster when we met. At least give it a shot with this Bumble girl if you're interested. Being present with someone can change a lot," I said.

"Okay, Miss Counselor, thanks for the tip," Zara joked.

The staff started to clear some of the tables and the place seemed to be turning more into a club.

As I tried to get the bartender's attention, Zara leaned over to me and loudly whispered, "By the way, I smiled at that guy in the white shirt and his friend. They keep looking. I think they're going to come over soon."

"How do you know they're interested in us? They're just standing there, and you always say that every guy wants us."

Zara pulled out one of the stools from under the bar and sat on it. "When someone keeps eye fucking you, I think it's pretty obvious. And they do. Guys don't come to clubs for the dancing or to invite you to play Monopoly. They see clubs as a mating ground," she said.

"Oh yeah, what about the guys who are taken?" I asked sarcastically.

"If they're in a club, they came to flirt and check out your ass. Anyway, have a look— he won't stop staring now. He must be summoning up all his courage," she said.

As I turned slightly and had another glance, I locked eyes with him. *Shit! He caught me.* I casually turned away, as if I hadn't really seen him. I decided to wait a few minutes and have another look. We locked eyes again. We stared at each other a little longer. This time, he broke eye contact first. An instant excitement rushed through me. Having been caught up on the same person for so long, I'd almost forgotten about this playfulness.

"And now that you know he's interested," Zara said smugly, "play hard to get."

"Why would I play games when I know he's interested? That's just ridiculous," I asked. I knew she was right, and I was already sort of doing that but failing miserably.

"Because you don't know what his intentions are. And stop looking at it so negatively. It's just understanding how courtship works. The less attention you give the hot ones, the more they want you. Make them feel a little insecure and you'll have them eating out of the palm of your hand. You need to stop being so nice and actually bruise their ego. Oh look, here he comes. I told you he'd come over soon," she laughed.

CHAPTER 2

DRINK?

"Are you serious? Do I look okay?" I asked.

"You look hot."

"Quick... how's my lipstick?" I asked under my breath.

"Everything looks great, babe. Don't stress."

"I'm going to the ladies' room. I'll be back in a minute," I said anxiously, not knowing if I would be able to hold a conversation. I didn't feel like myself.

Zara grabbed me and mumbled in my ear, "Oh, no you don't. You're staying here."

"I'm really not that interested. What am—"

"Hey, ladies, how are you?" he interrupted confidently as he put his hand gently on Zara's back. She slightly moved away from him.

He had these warm, brown eyes. I've always been more attracted to guys with darker features. Maybe it's because I have blue eyes and pale skin—you know, that whole "opposites attract" thing. Zara, on the other hand, is tan nearly all year round and has these big, hazel eyes that could suck anyone in. I eyed him up and down while I had the chance. He was taller than me, and I had heels on ... always a preference. He had a faint scar on his right cheekbone and another on his left eyebrow. He was beautiful but rough around the edges. He looked classy but a little bad at the same time.

"We're on a vacation in New York. How do you think we are?" Zara replied without hesitation and a little drunk. She has a similar pattern in attitude when meeting a hot guy for the first time, especially when she's had too much to drink.

He raised his eyebrows and smirked. "Well, you're a nice person. Does that usually work with guys you meet?" he asked sarcastically.

"Umm, yeah it does, actually," Zara answered back, smiling at him.

"Wow," he said, looking away for a moment.

I could tell this conversation was about to go from zero to a hundred very quickly. Unlike other guys, this one was not taking her shit from the start. I don't think she expected it. But knowing Zara, once she's challenged, she won't back down.

"You know they say that rudeness is a sign of insecurities. The rudest people are the most emotionally unstable," he continued.

Zara's face dropped, and there was an uncomfortable silence. No one spoke for a few seconds.

"We were all looking at each other from across the bar, so I thought I'd come and say hi. That's all," he said.

"I haven't been checking out anyone, so don't get too ahead of yourself," Zara replied, getting her back up.

"I came over very politely and asked how you were. There's no need for the ego," he said calmly.

"I don't need to hear this shit," Zara snapped.

"Look, you might be pretty, but that's no reason to show rudeness to someone who's been nice to you. And, holding that Givenchy doesn't make you classy; attitude does. Your rudeness might work with your other little boys, but I can see straight through it... sorry," he answered.

Zara looked at him like he had just stripped her bare and exposed her secrets to the world. "Excuse me? You don't even know me, so you can fuck off."

"You're right. I don't know you. I only know what you've shown me," he replied.

Zara raised her eyebrows and looked at me. "I'm going. You can stay if you want."

I was still trying to work out what the hell just happened. Zara stormed off in her tight white dress and brand-new heels. Not just any heels, her new Louboutins, which set her back a mere $870. I'm being sarcastic; $870 for me is like two weeks' wages, but it's not that much for Zara. That woman doesn't leave the house without a pile of cash. By the end of the night in her drunken state, it's usually falling out of her bag. I've basically known Zara my whole life (or for as long as I can remember). Her younger sister Chloe and I have been friends since we were kids. Last year, Chloe traveled to Sydney, Australia for a vacation and got offered a job. She's always posting pictures of the beach. She FaceTimed me last week while she was on her "daily coastal walk." She's such a lucky bitch.

Zara is six years older than me, and we definitely have a unique relationship. I think most people do with her. Zara's been really hurt in her past. She doesn't open up very often and won't show her vulnerabilities as much as I do. I guess it's a defense mechanism, one that's helped her get to where she is in her career. She owns a successful online marketing agency in San Fran ... that's where we live.

Zara once said to me, "I was hurt so much by my ex ... never again. I will never give up so much of myself again." I'm starting to understand what she meant. She wasn't one of those girls who had everything given to her on a silver platter. In fact, she was the opposite. Her father left when she was young, and she lived with her three siblings in the same one-bedroom apartment. Her mom couldn't afford to buy them enough food sometimes, so they lived on bread. She's worked so hard to get her company to where it is. She's not perfect and has problems like all of us do, but when it comes to the crunch, she always has my back. She's a tough-minded bitch with a soft heart. She's the epitome of the women's revolution: climbing the ranks when all the odds were against her. Sometimes her attitude is unbearable and slightly annoying, but she's my friend. Deep down, she has a heart of gold and would do anything for anyone. I have told her things that only my bedroom walls know about. I love her.

"Babe, *stop*. Just give me a second!" I yelled, quickly walking to catch up to her.

"I was only joking. He didn't have to be such an asshole about it," she replied.

"I agree, but emotions are high right now, especially because we've been drinking. But if you really want to leave, I will," I replied with a little hesitation. "And is everything okay with you?"

Zara stood there for a minute, thinking . . .

Then her energy seemed to be calming. "Yeah, everything's fine," she answered, looking away.

"To be honest, it doesn't seem that way. Are you gonna tell me?" I pushed.

"I don't know, okay. I've just been a bit stressed lately," she said, rubbing her forehead.

"Why? Do you want to talk about it?"

She took a deep breath and said, "It's just with work and stuff. I think I've been extra snappy with everyone. Fuck...I'm sorry. This is your vacation," she continued.

"It's both of ours. And I was sort of just starting to get into it before that little incident," I joked.

"I was a bit of a bitch to that guy, wasn't I?" she asked.

"If you want me to be honest, yeah, but what's new? I think you met your equal," I replied, laughing.

Just as I finished speaking, a security guard approached us. "Is everything okay with you girls?" he asked.

I didn't think I'd ever seen someone so big. I gave Zara a look to not tell the guard what had happened and make things worse.

"Everything's fine. Just girl talk, I promise," she said while giving him an innocent, flirtatious smile.

The guard walked back over to the corner of the dance floor and kept a close eye on us.

Zara took another deep breath. "All right, fuck it. Let's just stay."

We walked back over to the bar but away from that guy and his friend. The guy kept looking over for the next fifteen or so minutes then approached us again. I understood his stance with Zara, but at the end of the day, she's my friend.

"Hey, is everything cool?" he asked, looking at Zara.

"What's your name?" I asked him.

"Nick. And yours?" he replied, looking into my eyes. His energy completely drew me in. He seemed so strong.

"Amelia. Look, if you want to talk to us, apologize to my friend for the way you just spoke to her. If not, no hard feelings, but we'll be leaving it here," I said, trying to balance out the energy.

"I'm not a little girl. I don't need an apology. It's fine," Zara interrupted.

"No, you do. I shouldn't have said what I said," he quickly replied. "It was out of character for me. I guess I just got pissed off with what you said, and I went too far. I'm sorry if I upset you. Can we restart this whole thing?" he asked, putting his hand out to shake hers.

Zara looked away, thought for a moment, and then shook his hand. "My name is Zara. And don't worry. I'm not as sensitive as it seems.

"So, Nick, do you always walk up to girls in clubs and try to charm them?" she said jokingly.

"No, not quite. Do you girls want to come and grab a drink? They're on me. It's the least I can do." Just as he asked, his friend walked over. "And this is my friend Jordan. He's a bit more reserved, so take it easy on him," he continued, putting his hand on Jordan's shoulder.

"Well, he and Amelia will get along like a house on fire tonight," Zara whispered under her breath.

"Thanks for the great introduction, Nick. Girls, it's a pleasure. You both look beautiful," Jordan said.

"Thank you. That's really nice of you to say," I replied.

Jordan seemed really sweet, like the guy your parents would fall in love with. To be frank, Nick seemed like the type of guy who would pull your hair, slap your ass, and ... well, you get the rest, while Jordan seemed like more of the "making love" guy.

"Your charm isn't going to get you far, Jordan. You can get us that drink, though," Zara said in a lighthearted tone. I knew she wasn't ready to give away her attitude completely, but she was much more aware of it with Nick's masculine energy close by. A rare sight with Zara.

"Let's do it," Nick answered.

We all walked around to the other side of the bar, where less people were waiting in line.

"What would you like, man?" the bartender asked as he pointed to Nick.

"Girls … tequila shots and vodkas afterward?" Nick asked.

"Yeah, sure," Zara answered.

"Four Don Julio 1942 shots and four Grey Goose with soda and lime, please. And where are you from? I'm hearing an accent," Nick said to the bartender.

The bartender looked up and said, "London."

"Nice. I have a conference there soon. I'm thinking about staying for a few months."

"Yeah, cool. I'll be back by then, so I'm more than happy to let you in on a few good spots," the bartender said as he took a bottle from the shelf.

"I'd appreciate that. I'll grab your Instagram before I head off tonight and we can stay in touch," Nick replied.

As the bartender started preparing the drinks, Zara tapped Nick. "Conference in London? What do you do?"

"I'm a partner at Adam Steinberg's, but my two passions are photography and surfing," he replied.

Zara stood upright. "Isn't that the big law firm?"

"Yeah. We have a few bases around the world now. It's been a lot of hard work but equally a blessing."

"I know what you mean; business is never easy. I guess people just look at the lifestyle when someone is finally doing well and make their judgment on that. They don't understand the dedication behind it all," she replied.

"Well, yeah, it's easy to get caught up with the materials, but you have to stay grounded. We were always taught good morals growing up. I never really lived a sheltered life. I didn't have everything given to me, but I'm grateful for that. My parents gave me love, which was more important than anything," he said. "But regardless, when you're trying to get ahead in life, people will still judge. We all do it to some extent; it's human nature. You can't please everybody; you just gotta be yourself."

I was sort of listening to what they were saying but couldn't really relate. While I like my days in PR, I have never owned my own business.

Zara was watching Nick closely as he was speaking. "You look young to be a partner at a big law firm. How old are you, if you don't mind me asking?" she asked.

Nick grinned before answering, "Hmm, I have a feeling you don't believe I'm a partner. . . . I'm old enough."

"Fine, that's the last time I try to get a straight answer out of you," Zara joked.

"Well, to explain, I just think age doesn't matter right now, especially because it's so early in getting to know each other. Sometimes knowing someone's age too quickly creates unnecessary judgment. I prefer to get to know you, the person. I've personally met twenty-three-year-old women and thirty-five-year-old little girls, if you get my drift."

"Oh, trust me, I do, because I've experienced something similar with boys and men. But I just think a lot of experience and wisdom come with age."

"That's true, sometimes. I look at it a little differently, though."

"How so?" Zara asked.

"I feel like I'm being way too anal now. Sometimes I just look into things too deeply. I'm sorry," he said, laughing.

"No, it's fine. I want to hear," Zara responded.

"All right. Well, let's say there's one person in their twenties and another in their forties. The younger person has a particular experience, learns what they can from it, and changes their life because of it. The older person has many of those same experiences and keeps going around in a circle. Who would you say is wiser? Who are you more likely to take advice from?" he replied.

I think Zara's doubts were gone after he answered like that. While eavesdropping, I was thinking that he could have just told her his age and not made anything of it. But the other part of me liked the fact that he could have a conversation. He seemed wise, unlike a lot of other guys I usually meet.

"That's true. I guess it's not the number of experiences you have, but what you learn that matters," Zara added.

After the bartender finished pouring the drinks, Zara tried to pay, but Nick wouldn't let her.

Once he paid, we all grabbed a shot of 1942, said cheers, and slammed them down. Stupid me spilled a little bit on the bottom of my skirt. Lucky I was wearing black.

As we put the glasses back on the bar, Nick looked at me and Jordan. "Now, are you two gonna talk or just look around all night?"

Jordan gave Nick a death stare and finally faced me. "Sorry about that. He gets a bit out of hand sometimes."

"I can tell, but he's nice. What do you do?" I asked.

"I'm an accounts manager for a company here in New York, but I'm on leave right now. I just needed a break. So, why are you in New York?"

"Just to get away, to be honest," I replied. I kept looking over at Nick when Jordan was speaking. I could hardly concentrate on our conversation.

Don't get me wrong; Jordan was cute, but Nick was handsome.

"It's about a guy?" Jordan asked.

"Ahh, yeah. But I don't really want to talk about it right now," I replied. I was lying though; I did want to. That's all I've wanted to speak about. I wanted answers, and I wanted to get into a man's mind, to understand them more. I think a lot of the misunderstanding in the modern dating scene comes from not communicating properly. We don't speak; we don't even try to understand each other. And I'm not ignorant. I know I will never understand some people, but in general, there are answers out there when it comes to why men act the way they do.

Rachel's boyfriend, Paul, has definitely awoken me to some of those answers—including his opinion of what a "real man" is—but I'm committed to finding out a lot more, especially because of what's happened recently. I'm sick of guessing and coming back to the same point.

I waited for Jordan to probe . . .

[[To be continued.]]

CHAPTER 3

FIVE WEEKS EARLIER

8:33 a.m.

The light beaming through the window was so strong, it was piercing through my eyelids. I rolled around and buried my head into the couch. *I just want a good night's sleep.*

I must have left the TV on as well; I could hear the weatherman speaking in the background, "And for today, mostly sunny with possible showers in the evening."

I didn't want to get up yet, but I was busting to pee. I got off the couch and started walking across the room.

"Shit!" I yelled as I nearly fell flat on my face. I'd tripped over the empty bottle of champagne on the floor. I've got a habit of tripping over things, sometimes even my own feet. My friends used to call me "Kneelia" because I would most likely end up with grazed knees after a big night out.

The girls had wanted me to go out with them last night, but I'd just wanted to have a night in on my own. Sometimes I can't deal with the whole social thing. I want my own company, and I don't want to see anyone. I saw the bottle of Veuve on top of the refrigerator and just thought, *Fuck it*. Zara gave me some bottles that were left over from a work function. I was saving them to drink with Jay on my birthday, which is coming up next month. *That obviously isn't going to happen.* Do you know what's fucked? You speak to someone so much, and then they act like you never shared any real connection. I don't get it. But even though I got pretty drunk last night, I'm proud of one thing: I didn't text him. I was so tempted. I don't know where I got the strength.

I stumbled down the hall to the bathroom in my underwear. *The toilet seat is up. Paul must have slept over.* He's been here so often lately, sometimes

I feel like he lives with Rachel and I too. But I don't mind; I couldn't think of anyone better for her.

After I finished on the toilet, I walked back over to the basin to wash my hands and face myself in the mirror. My hair was a mess, and the left side of my face was creased from the grooves on the couch. I brushed my hair, rinsed my mouth, and went back down the hall to my bedroom. I put on the most comfortable tracksuit pants I could see and a baggy Adidas top I bought years ago.

"I'm sick of guys and their bullshit," I burst out to myself as I was getting changed. There are so many times when I have wanted to call people out on their crap, especially Jay, and haven't. I feel like I need to be myself and stand up for what I believe in more. But there's always that battle going on in my mind: should I stay silent or should I express myself? These days, it's like we're expected to accept people's ignorance and rudeness, and if we do express ourselves or call them out on it, we're the ones who are seen as crazy. We're all so scared to say what we want in case we get judged for it, or God forbid, it gets shared on social media.

It was even happening prior to meeting Jay. Guys I was interested in would message me and then play games. Sometimes I really felt like texting them, "Why the fuck do you message to meet and not follow through? What's the point of acting all interested and then disappearing? Grow up!" It's seriously just pathetic how some people act. If you don't want to meet, all good. I don't care. But don't say one thing and do another. And obviously, I don't text stuff like that. I know I'll regret it and don't want to stoop to their level, but geez, I've come close so many times.

Zara told me to go over to her house today and chat. She's been away for work the past week and waiting for an important delivery at home. I slipped on my sandals, grabbed the packet of cigarettes off the bench, and left. She lives only a few blocks away, so I took the backstreets to get there.

I arrived and buzzed her room number, 2112, from outside.

"You're late. You were supposed to be here an hour ago," Zara said through the intercom.

"It's Amelia," I replied.

"Shit, sorry. I thought you were the delivery guy. Have you had a coffee? I'm making one."

"Are you going to let me in or just speak to me from up there?" I said, hung over and tired.

Zara laughed and buzzed me in. I walked past the art feature in the middle of the foyer toward the elevators. They only finished building these apartments a few months ago. The scents of fresh paint and new furniture filled the air. There was something strangely nice about it.

As I walked through the front door of Zara's apartment, she passed me a mug. "Here, I just made you a coffee. Come drink it on the balcony, though; you need some vitamin D. You're white as a ghost."

We walked out and sat on her sun beds on a balcony that's bigger than my whole apartment.

"I feel sick to my stomach. I can't believe what just happened, and I can't stop smoking. Look, I even bought a packet," I replied.

"Why? What happened now? And what happened to your vape?"

"I needed a cigarette. The last week has been a roller coaster. So much shit has happened, I don't even know where to start. Do you think his friends are in his ear?"

"Tell me what happened," Zara pushed.

"Earlier in the week, I went on Facebook—"

"You checked his Facebook when I told you not to, didn't you?" she interrupted.

"No. I thought I'd stopped his statuses from coming up on my newsfeed. But I looked yesterday, and he uploaded pictures with his friends. The caption was 'At peace.' I can't even explain how I felt. I hardly even go on that shit Facebook anymore ... I shouldn't have checked it," I replied, gulping my coffee and lighting a cigarette.

"What a pig. He knew you'd see it. Maybe it was such a shock because you were holding onto false hope," Zara said.

"Maybe he didn't know I would see it; he doesn't use Facebook that much. And I was thinking that maybe he just meant 'at peace' about something else," I replied.

"Come on, Amelia. Stop making excuses for him."

"I'm not, but seriously, how do I know it's about me?"

"Well, why did it upset you so much?"

"Because I don't know; it could be. It's a possibility," I replied.

"In my opinion, he's just been a fucking coward about the whole thing. Come on, Amelia. I have to be upfront with you—it's the only way you're going to get over it."

I could feel the sun starting to warm my face. I got up and moved the chair into the shade. "Anyway, I decided to unfriend him after that. I was sitting in my room the other night speaking to my mom, and she convinced me to do it. It was so hard. I feel like that was a connection with him and now it's gone. I felt like I took part in cutting any hope there might be," I said.

"Good. You need to do that," Zara replied.

"But you won't believe what happened. I woke the next morning, and he had sent me a text saying, 'Why did you delete me off Facebook?' It was seven thirty in the morning. And he's been doing other weird stuff like still viewing my stories on Insta and even reacting to one. He's liking some pics that I post as well. And I don't know for sure, but I think he might be trying to make me jealous with some of his Snaps and Insta posts. I'm not checking them anymore. I muted them."

Zara sat up on the sun bed and leaned toward me. "Are you serious? What the fuck is wrong with guys these days? Where have all the men gone? And it's amazing how he can do all this shit now, but in the end, he was so distant."

"Yeah, I don't get it. He wouldn't reply to me all day because he was 'busy.' Now he seems to have the time," I replied.

"It was like me and Dave in the end. I'd message him and he wouldn't reply, but I'd see him active on Insta. He started saying he was always busy with work, but his Messenger would be online. It's garbage.

"Honestly, social media has become a way for people to send subliminal messages. We try to get someone's attention by liking their picture or make them feel a certain way by posting things ourselves. The times of openly expressing how we really feel to someone are going. It's time for all these hidden messages now. We're all getting weaker. It's like, if you want to text, text. If you want to call, call. Make proper contact. And if they make out they're interested and then don't respond positively when you actually reach out, FUCK 'EM!" Zara said.

"I don't get it, though. Why is he doing all this shit when *he's* the one who left *me*?" I replied, taking a drag of my cigarette.

"Because he thinks he can just pop into your life whenever he feels like it. On his terms. Fuck, he's so similar to Dave," Zara answered.

"What happened with Dave?" I asked.

"He just wanted it on his terms all the time. He got upset when he wanted to be friends and I said no. He was so selfish. It was all about him. I offered him everything. He rejected it, so in the end, he got none of me. I'm not a toy to be played with when someone feels like it. I've learned to be like this... it helps me not get taken advantage of," Zara said.

"Yeah, I just want people to be real and upfront with me. Stop the bullshit," I added.

"You've been honest, and your intentions have been pure. I don't think he showed you the real him. He showed you what he wanted you to see so you'd like him. I think there's another side to him that he hides from you because he knows you won't accept it. And I think that person is showing now.

His behavior's really inconsistent too, and that's scary in any kind of relationship. I think a lot of it has to do with his jealousy. It should never be this hard, especially so early on. I mean, you guys weren't dating for very long. Too many games," Zara replied.

"I wish I could just fast track it and get him out of my mind. It's like a poison. But to be honest, I feel a bit better when he reacts to my stories and whatever. I know it's bullshit contact, but it sort of makes me know he's still interested. I'd probably be much worse if he ghosted me. Look what happened with Chloe with that guy in Sydney. She told me that he literally went MIA on her. Blocked her and everything out of nowhere," I said.

"He was probably married or had a girlfriend. And anyway, it was better for her," Zara replied. "You know, to love the wrong person or to be obsessed with someone can be like a drug. Having a bit of it feels good at the time, but it's not good for you. They say if addicts just get over the hurdle with no drugs, they won't want it anymore. It's the same as this. You gotta cut the snake off at the head. Having absolutely no contact is the best thing for you. You really need to give it time to fade," she continued.

"Yeah, I guess," I replied.

"And to add to that, knowing that he's still on your Insta will affect what you post too. You won't be posting what you normally do. All your activity will have a hidden agenda," she added.

Zara stood and grabbed her sunglasses and the ashtray off the balcony ledge. "Here, use this," she insisted.

I went to take the sunglasses from her right hand.

"Not them, bitch, the ashtray," she joked.

"Did you get a chance to delete him, by the way? I don't want any of my friends having contact with him," I said.

Zara looked at me weirdly. "Yeah, of course I did, but why are you so anxious about it?"

"I just don't want him to know what we're doing and stuff."

"Fair enough, but it's not like we parade photos around anyway."

"I'd just prefer it," I replied. "And do you know what's even more annoying?"

"What?" Zara asked.

"I feel like I'm too extreme. I don't think I'm cut out to be with someone. I either love them too much or I just don't care. It's always one way or the other. Maybe I should've been less available to him. I should've made it harder for him to get my time."

"That's crap. If you can't act like yourself with someone you're seeing, then who can you with? You're just not cut out to be with a dickhead like him. Anyway, he wasn't even that good. I don't know what you saw in him," Zara said.

"I keep thinking about the good times we had. My mind keeps replaying them.

And with all this shit on my mind, it's hard to concentrate on important things," I replied.

"Storage almost full. I think it's time to delete the three thousand screen shots I've never looked at," Zara thought out loud, looking down at her phone.

"Are you listening to me?" I asked.

"Yes, yes, sorry." She came closer to my face. "Okay...you have to think of things you disliked about him. If you don't, it will drive you crazy. Eventually, this perfect image of him will start to crack and you'll feel a little better. You dodged a bullet with this guy, trust me. You might not see it now, but it's a blessing in disguise he left.

"I don't think you really want him back, even though you keep telling yourself you do. And besides, when you stop chasing them, their mind automatically starts wondering what you're doing. They wonder who you're with and whether you really needed them as much as they thought. And that's exactly what you want them to think."

"Won't that stop him from saying how he really feels? If I act like I don't care?" I asked.

"No, it won't. By not contacting him, he's starting to feel rejection. I bet it's the only reason he sent you that message ... his own insecurities, not because he genuinely cares. I know that's hard to swallow, but it's the truth. If he cared, he would be begging for you back. But I don't think he has that in him, and I think you deserve someone who does," she said.

"Yeah," I replied, finding it hard to comprehend.

"Amelia, look at me. Don't give him the satisfaction of knowing you still care. You showed him that in the past and he took advantage of it. He doesn't deserve to know. If you want some dignity and self-respect back, if you want him to think you're that strong girl he met, don't show any more weakness."

The sun started to go away, and the clouds were coming in. We took everything inside and sat on Zara's soft leather sofa.

"He must still care to a degree if he's doing these things. Why won't he just say it? Why the games?" I asked.

"I don't know. In my opinion, he's a weird one. I'm not sure what he'll do next. A lot of people are mentally 'not all there.' They've been hurt; they're insecure and scared to be themselves. They don't want to let people in. We've all created this vicious circle of everyone fucking over everyone. We're all making each other vulnerable. We're all scared to look too interested. We don't want to scare people off, but by tiptoeing around, we aren't being ourselves, and that's always a recipe for disaster. Then again, sometimes I feel like we're all hypocrites in the dating world."

"What do you mean?" I asked.

"Well, I'm guilty of acting interested in someone and then pulling away. We expect someone we like to give us a chance even though they're not interested. But we don't give people a chance that we're not interested in. Anyway, you have a lot of power back now that he's contacted last. You definitely have the upper hand," Zara answered.

"I know; I felt really good for a few days after he messaged. I felt like I had more power within myself again—"

"Oh my God, Amelia, what the hell did you do now? I told you, once he contacts you, not to contact him back."

"I didn't. I saw a photo of him come up on Insta. He was with these two girls. They looked like fake bimbos. He hates girls like that," I responded. "Shit, look at me. I was never the jealous type. I never cared about such petty things," I continued, remembering how chill I used to be.

Zara raised her voice, "No, he told you he hated girls like that. And I wouldn't stress. They're probably just friends from work or something."

"Well, there were two blondes on either side of him. Seriously, their hair was so fake it looked like it would glow in the dark."

"Yeah…and what did you do, Amelia?" Zara pushed.

"Well, I put my phone down, but when I checked my Insta a few hours later, I scrolled down and the same picture came up."

"Yes?" Zara probed.

I looked up at her. "The like heart was red. I must have accidentally liked it as I went to scroll down my feed. I didn't realize that whole time. I couldn't fucking believe it."

Zara's face dropped. "I don't know whether to laugh or cry. Okay, it's not that big a deal."

"Yes, it is! He's gonna think I'm some loser who's trying to act like I'm happy for him, some reverse psychology shit to bring him back. It looks so pathetic. And what am I going to do, unlike it and say, 'I'm sorry. That was an accident'?"

"No way! Don't contact again," she quickly responded.

"Babe, I don't know what it was. I don't know why he just pulled away on me. All these mixed messages are confusing. I think I just need closure, but I still don't have it. I still don't really know why," I said, walking around the room.

Zara picked up her coffee mug and a few other dishes around the house and went to the kitchen to wash them.

"Don't stress about the photo thing; we'll fix it," she said. "And you're right; not having closure is the hardest part, but I don't think we ever really get it this early, especially if we feel rejected. To me, closure doesn't come from knowing why the other person did it. Sometimes I don't think we ever get it from them, especially if someone has really deep issues they're scared to face—"

"I'm sure he had a few of those," I interrupted.

"Closure comes from knowing ourselves, knowing our worth, and finally realizing what we deserve. It's seeing the other person for who they really are, not who we've made them to be in our head. I don't think he really knows why he acts the way he does. I don't think he truly knows himself. If anything, your closure right now is knowing how confused he is. You want a man, not a little boy," she said.

"Honestly, it's like the roles have reversed. I used to be the cool one. So many people have said to me that you can lose who you are when you are infatuated with someone, but I think they forget to add that you can often become just like them."

"That's very true. Sometimes we take on their traits and then treat other people the way they treated us," Zara said.

I leaned back on her couch. "Did I not put enough effort in how I looked?" I asked. "He seemed cool with the natural, more laid-back look, so I kept it casual. I don't always put in as much effort or have a 'peachy' ass like some of these other girls out there. He always wanted to explore and push boundaries when we were having sex too, but I wanted to take it slowly so he would respect me and take me seriously. Maybe he thought I was boring."

Zara came back over and sat on the couch across from me. "Stop torturing yourself," she said. "You're trying to find any way to understand what happened, but you can't. You don't understand him because he doesn't understand himself. If he did, it would be clearer to you. There is nothing wrong with you. It's all in your head. Anyway, you shouldn't have to be someone else to suit anybody. You are who you are, and you don't give that up for anyone," Zara said assertively.

I took another sip of my coffee. "I know. I used to be so much more confident."

"Yeah, and you'll be even more confident when this is all over. Next time, don't sacrifice the person you are to suit somebody else's insecurities, jealousy, or lack of love. And stop letting your happiness be solely dependent on someone else's mood. That's how it got with you in the end. You changed. He brought out the worst in you," she said.

"That's not entirely true."

"Yes, it is. When he was giving you the cold shoulder, you'd always be agitated. You would snap at your mom and all of us. You were always down. But when he was happy, you were. He'd message you back and you'd be on cloud nine. Honestly, Amelia, that's not something you can build on. You were never the type to second-guess yourself. You're better than this," Zara added.

"I know I am, and that's the hard part," I said. "This whole experience is definitely filling up my Notes app, by the way. All these random thoughts have been pouring out of me," I said.

"Good; you should write down your thoughts. It's therapeutic. Maybe you'll turn them into a book one day," she joked, trying to make me laugh.

"Who knows what the future holds?" I said, looking outside.

"The future is what you make it. All I know is that you're about to find a lot of answers about dating and yourself through all of this. And that's gonna take your life to the next level. Ride it out," Zara answered.

"I hope so. Anyway, babe, I'm gonna take off," I continued as I finished my coffee.

"Are you sure?"

"Yeah, I'm gonna go for a walk around the park."

"In your sandals with socks on?" Zara asked, laughing.

"Yeahhh, fuck it," I answered back, laughing a little.

"All right, call me if you need anything," Zara said, hugging me and then walking me to the door.

June 15, 2019, at 10:48 a.m.

I see a beautiful guy holding a girl in his arms. It makes me wonder what's wrong with me.i do wonder how she gets a guy like that to love her so much. I feel like the guys I want just want sex from me

I hate when someone just ignores me.it's so rude.

-get cucumbers, cans of tuna, lemons, tampons, milk, toothpaste, moisturizer. Return headphones.

i know that "I'm not for everyone,"but I hate being rejected by someone I want. It makes me so frustrated. I don't know what's wrong with me

Every time he messages me, my heart skips a beat.

Every time I let someone in, they hurt me.

June 16, 2019, at 7:36 p.m.

I'm sick of random hookups.i want it to work out.

FUCK YOU FOR IGNORING ME

- Send tax information to accountant.

sometimes I wonder why it just can't be easier.
Why does it always have to be so hard?

I deleted his message thread from my
phone. I can't even see his name...it makes
me get that feeling in my stomach.

Watch Netflix documentary that
Rachel told me about.

What happened to romance? The
romance like they had in the 1940s?

To my future husband, wherever you are, whoever
you are...i want to spend my life with you, I want to
have kids with you, I want to travel the world with
you,i want to cry with you, laugh with you. I want
to lay down looking up at the stars and talk about
nothing with you. I want to get drunk and then
eat a kebab on the side of the road with you,not
care about my hair in front of you. I want to be
comfortable with you, I want to grow old with you.
I want to trust you. I want you to be in it forever.

CHAPTER 4

FAIRY TALE

Zara

I know of high school sweethearts or those who have been together forever, but I sure as hell am not one of them. Sometimes it upsets me to think that I'm someone who hasn't been able to hold a successful relationship yet, but I've learned a lot from my experiences, and I wouldn't trade that. Really, looking back, I wouldn't. I've traveled to many places around the world, met different kinds of people, and gone through the mental and emotional journey that it takes to build my own business. I have made mistakes and definitely dated them, but it's all a part of my life; it's all a part of my story. Call me a dreamer, call me an idiot, but I won't give up on the hope that one day a true, lasting relationship will meet me halfway. I put up a big wall sometimes, but I want to spend my life with someone special. I'm not afraid to admit that anymore.

When I give someone a chance, it's in the hope that maybe, just maybe, they will be the one I don't have to play games with. Equal attraction, equal love, equal goals. Wouldn't that be amazing? I know it's not all a fairy tale. It's real, with real problems, real feelings; that's a relationship. And the moment we think it's a fairy tale, we escape the reality needed to make it work or to deal with it when it doesn't. Where do fairy tales exist anyway? In a book? In a movie? A movie is only two hours long, for God's sake, not a whole lifetime.

Watching Amelia go through this has really woken me up. Her experience has made me reflect on my own life. And right now, not being emotionally attached to anyone has made me a lot more aware of the difference between love and lust. I'm still dating and getting sucked into the games from time to time, but no one really has my heart. I want to keep it that way until I make a decision not just based on irrational lust but real love. I felt like I'd been confusing what a real connection is. I'd go out with a really nice person on a date and then pull away. I used to think, *I just wasn't feeling it.* So, who did I feel more, those assholes that kept playing with me? Yeah, I might have thought they were hot, dressed well, or seemed cool, but where's the rest that makes a successful relationship? And looking back, was it true that I wasn't "feeling it" with these other people that would have done anything for me, or was I just being clouded by my desire to want someone I thought I couldn't have? Had I become that distant from my worth?

I see it with my friends, too: guys and girls. We have this overwhelming desire to feel wanted, to feel accepted. In a world that seems so connected, yet so far from having real communication, we crave it. Our high levels of insecurities are making us want it from people who don't even care about us. And things like Instagram don't help —we scroll away our self-worth by comparing our lives with pictures of perceived "gods and goddesses." What they don't show you is that they are just as fucked up as all of us. I know girls with hundreds of thousands of followers who are going through the same shit emotionally.

Before I started my venture in business, I got to a point where I was posting pictures in lingerie in front of my mirror. I always viewed lingerie as being sacred, something I'd only share with certain people. Before I knew it, I was sharing it with the whole world to get attention and likes. It wasn't reflecting who I really was as a person. A girl who I was dating at the time helped me see that there's so much more to who I am. That the first image I was portraying of myself was sexual. I never wanted that. I got to a point where I felt like I was sexualizing myself. And the reality was, I was attracting a lot more people in my life who only saw me from that point of view. I once said to my girlfriend, "Well, everyone else on Instagram is doing it" and then showed her profiles of some Insta famous girls. One day she grabbed my phone out of my hand and searched all these amazing women who are doing great things in their career and for the world. She showed me people like Ellen DeGeneres, Oprah, Emilia Clarke, and other actors, singers, business women, etc, who I looked up to. One by one, I noticed they weren't posting pictures like that at all. It was just a big wake up call.

I know everyone is different and I'm not hating on anyone. It's cool if some girls can post things like that and feel comfortable, but personally, it wasn't me. On a deeper level, getting more likes from those kinds of pictures didn't make me feel more empowered or confident about myself; they made me more self-conscious and insecure. It was short-term satisfaction but had a greater negative impact on my mind. When my next post got less than the last, I would raise the bar on what I was willing to share just for "recognition." It all started by seeing people who I was interested in, liking pictures of girls who were posting stuff like that. I thought I had to be the same.

We get caught up posting what we think other people will like instead of things we actually like. Makes me wonder who our Instagram profiles are actually for. Most of us are losing our identity and our individualism. And it's not like I don't still post sexy pictures or show my body sometimes, but there's a limit now. As a woman, I want to be known as more than that. I finally want to be me, not anyone else.

For a long time too, when I slept with someone or was intimate with them in any way, I felt more vulnerable toward them. My mind started thinking that I wanted them more. I felt like they thought poorly of me and got the wrong impression. That's why I try to be more selective now. I can't take the risk of being sexual with someone in the hope that more will come of it and then them never speaking to me again. It made me feel like shit. I'd always regret it. And if I am sexual now with someone I'm not seeing exclusively, I don't expect anything. Sometimes I can be very sexually driven, and knowing what I'm getting myself into before I commit to it has helped me feel more comfortable. I also had to accept that sometimes those who ignore my offer of love and care are highly insecure themselves. It's not rejection, and in a lot of cases, they end up with someone who isn't half the person I was to them.

When I get burned by people who don't really care about me, I reflect on those who were genuine. Those who I felt comfortable with and didn't have to walk on eggshells with. That was real. I should've given more of my time to them. Being compatible with someone isn't always about the obsessive feeling I initially get; I realize that now. It isn't always waiting for their text, wondering what they're doing all the time, or chasing because they're running. That's not being genuinely interested in who they are; that's being fixated on trying to force an energy to sync when it doesn't.

If it's genuine, it's not so anxious; it's not so intangible. Lust is quick to assume and tormenting to the mind. It doesn't truly understand the other and makes irrational decisions that generally make no sense. It's fake; it's surfaced. With lust, you can never really be comfortable being yourself. And yeah, of course I need to be attracted to someone to be with them, but if it's only that, I find myself ignoring the fact that I'm not really connecting with them, and that's wrong.

Real love feels better. It's more available. It's long conversations. It's feeling like you can call that person at any time of the day, but more importantly, not being scared that you'll look desperate in the process. I think I need to keep going on dates with people who are genuinely interested and stop self-sabotaging. I don't want to mistake kindness for weakness anymore. I don't want to see them as less desirable because they're giving me attention. That's what's real. That's when you can lie in bed with someone and feel safe, secure, and build a life with them. I don't want to put those who don't give a shit about me on a pedestal anymore, as hard as it might be. If there's anyone who deserves less of my attention, it's them.

CHAPTER 5

I FEEL

Amelia

When it comes to dating, I seem to be going in a circle. The ones I want don't want me, and the ones who want me, I don't want. It's the same scenario over and over again. I feel like two people never remain on the same level these days—their "wants" change so rapidly. I've tried to look at it positively, but when you keep putting your heart out there and nothing comes of it, it's a little hard. And the most frustrating thing is, even though I shouldn't want some of these guys who screw me over, I'm still drawn to them. I keep trying to convince myself that I shouldn't want someone who doesn't want me, but my emotions keep getting the better of me. I know deep down that I should be stronger than this. I know that I need to close the door and accept that my love wasn't appreciated. Not because it was wrong, but because I gave it to someone who couldn't understand it. I know I went too deep in my emotions for him. I know that I surrendered my power, my trust, and my mind to him. I fell. And I'm not sure we should "fall" for anybody now. Why do we have to fall? I want to stand next time I love someone. I want to be stronger.

Looking back, I guess it was ignorant of me to trust someone with my emotions so quickly. I went too fast in my mind. I ran when I should've walked. And even though I know what's logically correct, my mind still plays around with me. I wonder whether he'll treat another girl the way I wanted him to treat me, whether he'll want to spend time with her the way I wanted him to spend time with me. I feel like all the guys I've ever truly desired, even from my past, are willing to give it all to another girl but never to me. To some extent, it makes me feel unworthy, and that vulnerability does lead to new people I meet. It's that fear of opening up and being hurt again. I mean, who do we trust? Whether they're short-term passings with people that don't go the way I want or long-term relationships that end, I've noticed that the impact they have on my emotions can be the same. When I'm not at peace, I find myself latching onto people I like but who aren't giving me the same attention.

I'll be the first to admit that there are moments when I have this overwhelming desire to have more control in the situation, to regain some dignity. I know it's probably my ego that's making me think like that, but right now, it's the truth. These days, it's like I need to be the one who decides to pursue someone or not. When that's taken away from me by someone who has led me on, it sort of makes me anxious. And I believe that comes from insecurities and emotional instability. It comes from being fucked around so many times. And I'm not like this all the time. Usually, I'm a happy person and try to keep a positive mind-set, but sure enough, every now and then, I meet someone who makes me swallow the advice I would give to anyone else. Old scenarios repeat themselves, just with a different person. I start obsessing over someone I don't even really know. As much as I want to see the situation clearly when I'm lusting over someone, I can't. All logic and rational thought get thrown out the window.

Sometimes I find myself writing emotional texts to people (either out of anger or hurt) then contemplating whether I should actually send them. I'll think of all these things I want to say, hold back from sending, backspace and edit the text five times, hold back even harder, and then get weak and push send. I try to convince myself to send it by saying, "I should always express myself no matter what" or "Maybe if I explain my point of view and how I'm feeling, they'll care." Needless to say, most times I don't get the reaction I want from someone who didn't give a shit about me in the first place. And yep, it makes me feel like even more of an idiot. I've been there so many times, I'm deeply questioning the modern dating scene and what it represents. I've also realized I'm not the only one. The more I speak to people about my situation, the more I see how common it is. We're all confused. It's like, historically, we're at a standstill when it comes to relationships. We don't know which way to go or how to act. And truthfully, I think most times we don't even know what we really want … we just seem to know what we definitely don't want.

We're part of a generation that can have anything at the click of a button— clothes, movies, information, and we expect that from love. We're impatient when it comes to getting to know someone. We want to know pretty much right away whether we could be with them. I must say I don't think I give people much of a chance in the beginning. A few false moves on the first date, and they're out as a possibility. Well, to be honest, sometimes it doesn't even get to the first date. I'm strange too—there are times when I think I really want someone, but then when they give me a lot of attention, I don't want them anymore. *Maybe I'm the messed-up one, creating this recurring instability.* We want someone when we want them, and when we don't, we don't. It's sort of sick. Most people look for the closest exit when things aren't working out because they can just replace someone with the next swipe. We're so disposable, so replaceable. The fight to make a relationship work seems to be rarer with each generation.

Recently, my mom said something to me that I loved. She said, "You have to stop expecting people who don't love themselves to love you the way you love them." It's true. I had found love within myself. I knew how to give my full self to someone when I made the commitment. But I have to accept that not everyone understands how to love as I do. A lot of these guys I thought I'd wanted hadn't found love for themselves yet. How could they possibly understand the love I was ready to give?

People say to me, "You shouldn't feel like this over someone else; no one should take up that much of your thinking." But I think they forget how much they think about someone they like. It's always okay to look at things from the outside and judge, but when you're in it, it's just not that easy to switch off. I wish it was. And it doesn't make me a weak person because I can't be positive or in control all the time—I'm learning that. There are stages when I feel lost with my career, sad for reasons I don't really understand at the time, and of course, emotionally unstable when someone has just screwed me around. I'm not always going to pretend I'm happy when I'm not. I did let my guard down. I let him in.

Some people also say that it shouldn't affect me as much because I didn't know him very long, although I've been with guys for much longer, and it didn't have the same impact this did. You know, that impact where you constantly excuse them for replying to your text a day later or forgive them for not replying at all. That impact where you feel good if they're giving you attention but feel like shit when they aren't. That impact where you're constantly looking to see if they liked your picture on Insta. It almost doesn't matter who else liked it if they don't. I don't think how long you've known them has much to do with it. It's the way you feel about someone; it's how someone makes you feel. It's how much you put in with your mind and heart that matters. It's where you are in your life. No one likes to invest in something and not have it go the way they want.

Logically, I think I know exactly what I want in a partner, but in reality, can I really help who I fall for? When someone comes along and grabs my attention, it's hard to let go. You want to trust them; you want to have faith in human beings. Whether it's right, wrong, or stupid to feel for someone you haven't known for long, it doesn't make the pain any less real when you feel rejected, when you feel unwanted. If I'm an idiot for allowing myself to feel emotions, then it's a tag I'll gladly take.

CHAPTER 6

THE SPELL

Before I met Jay, I had been on a spiritual journey (not that it ever ends, obviously), and I found out a lot about who I was. It took me a long time to discover my essence, but when I did, I was ready to give that wholeheartedly to someone I thought deserved it. Sometimes I wonder whether the love I found within myself was a burden. Because of my soft heart, I excused things that didn't sit well with me, like getting a call back hours later or getting short replies to my texts that didn't answer my questions properly. In my opinion, he also hung out with these girls from work too much. I wasn't the type not to let him be friends with girls he knew, but I think there's a limit and a level of respect that should be met.

Apparently, they were always working on projects together. He works for an accounting firm. But when he's out having drinks with them and hasn't even called me back—I'm sorry; that's bullshit. I wasn't asking for much. I always backed down after I brought these things up with him because I would hear the same story, "What's the problem? I was gonna call you back. You don't trust me … I'm not doing anything wrong … chill." It made me feel like I was being too hard on him and looking into things too much.

Is keeping a guy on his toes the only way to keep him interested? Should I be the one who's less invested? I'm so involved in my thoughts that I feel I overanalyze everything. I've learned that even the most self-aware people can succumb to heartbreak; that's how powerful it is. They say love is blind, but I saw everything. I just chose to turn a blind eye to things because, when I love someone, it has no boundaries. Maybe people who know what they have to offer are too loving, too understanding, and too caring to be with someone. I'm too forgiving. Maybe I have to be more of a bitch. I feel like I keep attracting guys who need to learn something.

My auntie said that Jay has probably learned a lot from me and looks at me in a really positive light. I don't know how that's good for me, though.

I have soul searched in the past. I know that love for myself is the ultimate aim and that my thoughts predominantly control my emotions, but this is life, and it just isn't that simple. Now sometimes I see characteristics of him in other people or find myself talking to him when I'm all alone. I could be driving the car, sitting in my bedroom, or going for a walk, and I say things to him even though he's not there. It's usually only through my thoughts, but at other times crazily out loud. The other day, I got caught "talking to him" by the driver in the car next to me, so I had to make out like I was speaking through Bluetooth. I was angry and saying, "You don't want to see me? Are you fucking serious? Who do you think you are? Don't worry. One day, a girl will screw you over, and you'll regret not appreciating me," or along those lines, anyway.

This whole experience has even forced me to do other weird shit that I never thought I would do. Last week, I googled "how to get someone to desire you again." Everyone seems to be saying the same thing.

Their advice was to "not contact at all and focus on myself." This is also really embarrassing to admit, but a few days after the breakup, I sort of considered putting a spell on him. It sounds so pathetic and desperate, I know, but I read somewhere about this girl putting a spell on a guy she wanted, and he came back more frantic for her than ever. It actually worked for her. And I was so hurt and frustrated at that moment, I was almost willing to try anything. I know it's creepy to be looking for spells on the Internet, but when I came across them, I found one that seemed okay. It doesn't harm him; it just makes him think about me more. You have to get a candle, needle, and do some little ritual while saying,

> Needle in the flame, Needle in the fire,
> Pierce his thoughts. Make him writhe, agonize,
> Until his heart comes back to me.

Zara called me a desperate freak and nearly fell off her chair in laughter when I told her about the spell. I must be honest. I did feel like a bit of a psycho, so I didn't go ahead with it in the end. And I think Zara forgets the stuff she did when she was obsessed with the last guy. She'd call me twenty times a day and speak about the same thing. She was like a broken record on repeat. Also, if there was a medal for being the biggest online stalker, she would've gotten it.

My friend Rachel has a softer approach with me than some of my other friends do. Don't get me wrong; Zara's energy is well-needed, but Rach just comforts me at times. We have lived together for the past two and half years, and I'd be lost without her. She's strong, intelligent, and in touch with herself spiritually. There's this beautiful aura around her; I feel it as soon as she walks in the room. She usually has a deep perspective on things. She knows her self-worth. I've been like a pet lately, just waiting for her to walk in the door so I can chew her ear off.

Ideally, I'd love to stop all this hidden bullshit between Jay and me. I just want to pick up the phone and ask him how it got to this, but I don't feel comfortable anymore. It's weird. It's like he's a stranger now, so close in my mind, yet so far from my actual life. I wish I had the courage to call him, but then my mind starts wondering if I would give up more of my dignity by telling him how I feel. *Would he even answer my call?* You know, I never would've dreamed of having this uncomfortableness with him. Out of all people, not him. We were so cool and relaxed with each other from the start. I remember his contagious smile and humble personality when we first met. When he smiled, so did everyone else around him. I now question if it was his insecurities that I mistook for humility. Was it really a lack of inner confidence or deeper issues that he didn't show me? I think so now, but I could only see the best in him. His dress sense was amazing, too. Jay was just a really cool guy.

I remember the times when we would both leave work early so we could spend all day and night together. The days when we would go lie at the park, look into each other's eyes, and talk about everything for hours. I remember how his hair used to look when he would wake in the morning. It was so scruffy, yet so sexy. I remember the times we used to pillow fight in my bedroom or when he looked at me from the corner of his eye with that cheeky smirk. Those times when he would tickle me so hard I'd fall to the floor. He made me feel like a kid again and have that "young love" feeling. That love when you're completely in the moment, when you could just be your stupid self and let go. That love that was crazy but free.

He was so supportive of everything I wanted to achieve as well. I didn't care about getting expensive gifts or anything like that; it was the small things that made me love him. The way he held me, the way he gently stroked my forehead while looking into my eyes. He cared about me. People can say what they want, but I know it was real because I felt it. And what would life be if every time I felt something with someone, I denied it?

Through this whole situation, I've been really vocal to my friends and family. And most times, I've been vocal about the bad parts, so I don't blame them for only seeing that. But I have experienced a different side to him. I don't know what the fuck's gone wrong now. Usually I do, but this time, I honestly don't. I know he was going through a lot with his family and his career in the end. Maybe he's just really confused about what he wants at the moment. And that's not me making excuses or being in denial; it's me being realistic. I understand that matters of the heart aren't always black and white. There's a lot of gray. People aren't always certain at every moment of their life. I'm not an idiot. I've felt love for people in the past, and I know when we share something.

I guess there are parts of me that believe the person I invested in is still the beautiful person I met. That the person I fell for wasn't just a projection of some perfect image I created in my mind. I don't want to believe that I only saw on the outside what I yearned for on the inside. I don't want to believe it was all fake. I'm not selfish. I didn't just date him to fulfill my own emotional gaps. I saw great qualities in him. Unlike others, I don't just give up on someone so easily.

CHAPTER 7

THE CALL

I heard my phone ringing faintly. I searched in and around my bed but couldn't find it. *I left it in the kitchen.* I quickly ran and saw it on the table.

"Private number." *I wonder if it's him.*

"Hello?"

"Hey baby, how are you?"

"Seriously, why is your number on private? You know I hate answering them. Why would you do that?" I said.

"Can you please relax, Amelia? I'm calling from Aunty Kat's house phone," my mom replied.

"I've been trying to call you all day," I said, frustrated.

"I know. I was at the clinic. I couldn't answer," she replied.

I went back to my room and lay on my bed. "I'm so sick of being anxious, Mom. I just feel unsettled. It's with everything … my career, guys, living in this city," I said.

"I think you really need to see someone. Maybe it's not good just to talk to me."

"Why would I see a psychologist when you are one? And really, I don't need a psychologist. I need a mom, so can you just be there for me?"

"You know I'm here for you no matter what, but I'm still going to tell you what I've learned over my professional years and as your mother who has been through relationships. He's not the one for you, Amelia. I saw it for a while but didn't want to say anything to upset you. Sometimes I wish I had, and that's my mistake."

I could hear my Auntie Kat yelling in the background, "Screw him! He doesn't deserve you!"

"Why is everyone saying that? I thought everyone liked him. You and Dad seemed to get along with him," I replied.

"We did like him, but he was very different. You are close with your family, and even though your father and I aren't together anymore, our family is still very tight. He had no real relationship with his parents and, in my opinion, spoke quite disrespectfully about them."

"Yeah, I know all that, and that's why I feel like I need to help him, Mom. He doesn't know what he's doing. He pushes people away who love him the most. Maybe he never felt worthy enough. He'd always make comments like, 'I can imagine how many guys would want you' or 'Why would you want to be with me?'" I said.

"He knows exactly what he's doing—stop kidding yourself. You know since it happened I've been there for you, even when you call me in the middle of the night, but I won't lie to you. You're my daughter, and if I have to shove the truth in your face then I will," my mom said. "He's an asshole and a coward. He said he couldn't see you anymore in a text message when he was on a vacation with his friends. You would have done anything for him, and when you think about it, what did he do for you? You will meet someone one day who appreciates the beautiful girl you are, but he was toxic," she continued passionately.

"I hate the fact that I have to hate him to move on," I said, confused.

"You don't have to hate him; you have to face the truth about the type of person he is. I know it's hard, but you have to wipe away those tears and be strong."

I wiped my eyes and composed myself. "It just hurts me, you know? I don't even feel comfortable enough to talk to him. And when I meet other guys now, all I do is compare them to him. I don't connect with them like I did with him."

"It's just because your perception is flawed by your emotions. And you have to start looking at things these new guys have that Jay doesn't, because I can assure you, he's not this amazing guy you keep making him out to be. You know what a big problem is with you girls these days?"

"What?" I asked.

"You don't know how to pick them. I'm not sure what you look for, but it doesn't seem to be making you happy."

"Okay. But even though I see what these other guys have, I don't get the same feeling as I did with him."

"Getting your heart broken is one of the most painful things in life…it's your sense of direction changing. It's your future being smashed into a million pieces. To lose all direction is a helpless feeling. Without having something to look forward to, you have no incentive to do purposeful things. But your main aim now—and it will take time—is to rebuild a future in your mind without him. Once that starts to become clearer, you will think of him less. I promise. It's a step-by-step process."

"But I just don't understand why a few days before he stopped talking to me, he said he misses me," I said, remembering the text message.

"He's very troubled, baby, but he's still aware of what he's doing to you. He knows you still want him; you made that obvious by pouring out your heart to him. I read this thing on Instagram the other day—"

"Yeah, what?" I asked.

"It said, 'No matter how attractive a person's potential may be, you have to date their reality.' I know your head is going around in circles hoping that he'll change or 'wake up,' but he knows what he's doing. He is very manipulative and broke you down bit by bit. If you ask me, he's very narcissistic."

"That's a little extreme, Mom," I said.

"No, it's not; it's quite common, actually. I would ask him how he was, but he would never really ask back. He would speak about himself freely but never really cared about others. Even your friends said that. And on the odd occasion when he did ask, it felt like I was speaking to a statue, to someone who wasn't really interested. I mean, he hardly involved you in his life either. He hardly ever invited you out to mingle with his friends. It's like he had two separate lives," she said. "I don't know, Amelia. There just wasn't much warmth there. He lacked empathy, and I think that's obvious now. Look, I'm not saying he's a bad guy or even that he's doing it purposely to hurt you, but he has a long way to go to find himself. The truth is, he may never. You have to come to terms with that. This is who he is," she continued.

"Maybe you're right. Maybe I was wrong about everything. Maybe he never cared at all. Honestly, I don't know what to think anymore."

"It's not to say he never cared, Amelia. I don't think that's the point here," Mom replied.

I walked over to the sink to get some water.

"Anyway, what do you have planned today? I saw your post on Instagram the other day at the park. Where was—"

"Mom, wait a sec. I have another call," I interrupted. "Oh my God."

"What?" she asked.

"It's him."

"Who?"

"Jay. Fuck," I said, finding it hard to contain myself.

"Don't answer," Mom quickly responded.

I let it ring a bit, contemplating what to do. "I have to. Hold on," I said to her.

"Hello?"

"Hey, how are you?" he asked.

"Hey! I'm really good. How are you?" I answered enthusiastically, masking how I felt.

"I've been pretty sick, to be honest; I was in bed all last week, so I haven't been doing much. How have you been? Have you been okay?" he said, sounding depleted.

"Yeah, I've been great. It's been a while since we've spoken, stranger. It was one of the girls' birthdays from work over the weekend, which was fun," I replied, lying. I'm not sure where that came from.

"Oh, nice. I'm just heading down to your side of town, stuck in traffic. How's your family and stuff?" he asked casually.

"They're good. I'm going to see my little cousin tomorrow."

"Oh, yeah... that little monster who used to jump all over me. He's a cutie. What are you up to now anyway?" he asked.

"Not much, just chilling," I said, sort of waiting for him to ask to catch up.

"Oh, sorry. Did I catch you at a bad time?"

"No, it's fine, but can we chat sometime soon?" I said, remembering the advice I read on the net. *Be the one to end the call.*

"Okay cool, well, yeah, just called to see how you are," he said.

"Oh, thanks. Let's chat soon. Have a good day."

"You too," he responded.

I switched calls back to Mom. "Mom, are you there?"

"Yes. What happened?"

"I can't believe he just called me. He didn't sound like himself, though...he sounded really down. I think he's starting to feel it," I answered.

"I wouldn't put money on that. He probably just wanted to know if you're still pining for him. I hope you didn't sound upset," Mom said, caution in her voice.

"I think he wanted me to ask him to meet up, but I didn't. I acted happy and confident. Do you think I should have asked if he wanted to meet?"

"Well, even if he was waiting for you to ask to catch up, that's cowardly. And if you asked him to catch up, he would have brushed it aside. I have no doubt about that. That would've been enough satisfaction to know you still care. Good girl—I'm proud of you. He doesn't deserve to hear you feeling needy anymore, but you also have to stop analyzing every single word he says."

"I actually feel good, Mom. It's like a weight has been lifted off my shoulders," I said. For the first time in a while, I felt free from my tormenting thoughts.

"Anyway, Rachel has just walked through the door, so I'll speak to you later," I continued.

"Amelia, listen to me. You can know someone isn't right for you and still be weak toward them. That's all it is now."

"Yeah, okay, Mom, I've gotta go. I'll speak to you soon," I answered.

June 19, 2019, at 4:02 p.m.

Sometimes I get lost in my visions of being with someone. My mind drifts off… I feel their love. I even smile at the thought. It feels so real sometimes.

  i want that spark. I don't want to settle for someone if it's not there. But every time it comes, it seems to go. People will tell you that you have to settle with someone you are compatible with,someone who is good to you. But you know what? without that spark, without that connection, I don't think I can settle. If it doesn't exist, if it's only a fairy tale, then I will be lonely till the day I die.

  i hear all these speakers on social media saying, "You don't need someone to be happy,we are women, etc etc." Yeah, that's cool, I might not "need" one, but in reality I do want someone special to share my experiences/life with.

June 20, 2019, at 10:04 a.m.

What do you listen to, your mind or heart?
Sometimes they feel like enemies.

If you've been hurt, it means you've lived. You opened
up, you allowed yourself to be free in those moments,
without barriers. You let go.and even though now
you might feel pain…imagine if you never allowed
yourself to feel. What would be the point of life?

Sometimes they're too nice. They're too
clingy. Maybe the thrill of the chase does
draw me in more than it should.

   stop being weak and second guessing
what you initially wanted to say. Be strong and
stick by the emotions you felt at the time

CHAPTER 8

WOMAN

Mom

I'm a fifty-two-year-old woman. I've experienced and seen a lot. And I can tell you, nowadays, substance and depth are underrated when looking for a partner. Most people are looking for some epic spark, but I've found, in most cases, it fizzes out when it's lit too quickly. What happened to focusing on real conversation? Being able to connect with someone? To understand them—their fears, their loves, their goals? To know what they are feeling without even saying anything? Yeah, that takes time, but it also takes an understanding of what someone really wants. Girls, including my daughter, need to ask themselves, "What do I really want?" If that's not clear, they'll just latch onto anyone who grabs their attention … or to the one who isn't giving them enough. They have to stop being so subconsciously desperate. That's what I call it, anyway. They're just so ready to give themselves to the first hot guy who comes along.

These girls need to wake up and understand what a real man is. A man has respect and integrity. He has self-awareness and will fight to give the people he loves the best opportunity in life, not make them constantly feel insecure. So many girls ignore gentlemen who actually want to get to know them and are giving them the attention they deserve as a woman. Instead, they chase assholes time and time again. I can't get my head around it. And then they sit in my office and ask, "Why does this always happen?" when things don't work. Of course, there are a lot of guys who manipulate and treat women like crap, but we have to take back control. We have to choose men who respect us for the amazing beings that we are. The more love we find for ourselves, the more we realize that. A big lesson I learned was that, most times, people will treat you the way you allow them to treat you. It took me years to take the reins back on my life.

Girls need to take a deep breath, put all the garbage aside, and actually get to know someone before they commit with their mind and heart. They need to understand what it takes to build a life with someone. To accept that compatibility is as important as attraction. When they meet someone new, they have to ask themselves, "What energy is he giving off in regard to his intentions? How does he react to things that are important to me? What are his morals and values? What do I need in a partner?" They don't have to sit there like a strict schoolteacher, but they need some idea. And the hardest part is not lying to themselves and facing the truth when things don't add up. No one is perfect, but there needs to be some awareness of what we need in a partner.

There was a time when I ignored what I needed and went through multiple failed relationships. Amelia's stepdad and I met fifteen years ago, and I'm still happily married to him. He's the type of man who always looks out for our best interest while we look out for his. We support each other, not tear each other down. When I met him, I had been through enough to know what I wanted in someone, and I wasn't willing to give it up. I was thirty-seven then, but younger girls can come to their senses a lot earlier by learning from their own or others' mistakes.

Amelia fell in with Jay so blindly. And I know she's young and still learning, but I don't want her to keep going around in circles her whole life. She has to accept that only someone who is unfulfilled can keep another person on a string with no intention of being with them. To deliberately mislead someone who likes you is a very low act. As human beings, we have to be aware of and take responsibility for how our actions affect others, even unintentionally. But when it comes to narcissistic people—which Jay was, in my opinion—the lack of empathy toward others is greater. He was able to shut off his emotions more easily. He was able to do what suited him regardless of who was being hurt in the process.

Those with high narcissistic traits tend to act ignorant toward the way they make others feel. They don't care how they make you feel because they want to feel good about the situation, and they will go to any measures to achieve that. They will manipulate you, give you false hope, and play mind games. They feel good knowing other people desire them, and if they have to, they will make you insecure to achieve that. They usually have double standards; what's good for them is usually not good for their partner.

They won't praise you often but will speak freely about their own achievements. They're rarely proud of your accomplishments, even if they might portray that on the surface. A lot of times, they feel inadequate and get jealous. It can feel like you're competing with someone who is meant to be your lover or friend. They will do weird things when you stop talking and give you mixed messages. They also have unrealistic expectations. They create this perfect image in their head of someone they like, but when that person doesn't live up to that image for one moment, they start to turn. Narcissistic people rarely admit their own faults; it's easier to blame others than to face their own demons. They're also generally full of excuses.

I could tell Jay self-sabotages things that are great in his life. He pushes away people who love him most. It could be because he feels a parent didn't love him, a toxic relationship he was once in, etc. When Amelia's father and I broke up, I made a conscious effort always to tell her that her father loved her. If she didn't see her father as a positive role model, she could hate men for the rest of her life. I was aware of that.

It's sad whatever has made Jay like this, but he is breaking down Amelia's mind in the process, and that's not acceptable. His energy is making her insecure and anxious. We often feel like we need to fix people like that, like we have to help and nurture them. And that's the situation Amelia has found herself in. What she doesn't realize yet is the only way she can help is by not giving him the attention he constantly seeks. By not giving it, we force people like Jay to turn inward. They have to look in the mirror.

They say that you can only help the willing, and in a lot of cases, people don't think they need help nor do they want it. In my opinion, she needs to get as far away from his energy as possible. I know he'll continue to give her false hope, emotionally abuse her. Jay's fulfillment is solely dependent on the attention he gets from others, and right now that's from Amelia. He doesn't know how to make himself happy. As soon as she gives him the attention he needs, he'll be gone again. That's why he keeps coming back in spurts. He doesn't commit; there's no need for him to do so. He can have peace by knowing she still wants him and can do what he wants on the side as well.

People can say it's the way she allows him to make her feel. Her feelings are solely her responsibility, but let's be real for a minute; people can impact the way we feel. We're all connected. So, she has to ask herself if this is the kind of guy she wants around her. A real man wants to protect his partner's emotions, not constantly see them hurt. They don't want to see them being down and put the blame on them. To me, a big reflection of someone's character is how they treat you when you're vulnerable. He took advantage of her vulnerabilities and made her feel scared to be herself. That's not a relationship. It's not even a friendship. It's nothing but a sad game. More people these days need to understand what it means to make a commitment to somebody and stop being half in, half out.

I hear people giving advice all the time and saying it wasn't meant to be or one day you'll find the one. I think a lot of that advice is untrue because it takes our choice out of the situation. If there is "the one" out there for everyone, then everyone would be living happily ever after, and we all know that isn't the case. At the end of the day, we choose who we dedicate our time to and who we allow in.

CHAPTER 9

EMPATHY

I went to the fridge and got out last night's Thai leftovers. "It's just taking time to get back to my old self," I said to Rachel.

"You don't need to get back to your old self. You need to build a new self with the new knowledge you have about human beings. You know I've always told you to go at your own pace and feel the emotions you have to feel. You don't need to hate him, but you do need to realize that, in the end, people like him don't lift you up," Rachel said, sipping on her tea and picking at my food.

"I know. I think you understand me the most. I feel like everyone else is trying to make me hate him to move on."

Rachel took a seat on the chair across from me and said, "It's so easy to hate, but that isn't going to heal you properly. It can actually keep torturing you. Some people hold on to that poison forever, and it affects everything they do in their life. It turns them into the people they despise."

"I'm just so fucking angry with what's happened sometimes. I'm angrier at myself for allowing someone to treat me like that. I even stopped talking to Chris for him," I said.

"You should call Chris and explain. I'm sure he understood why, but I don't think he was happy about it," Rach answered.

When I'd finally decided to stop talking to my friend Chris, I knew I had lost part of my soul. I tried to make myself believe I was doing the right thing, but a part of me left that day. I could tell Jay was jealous of Chris. It bothered him that we still spoke sometimes. I met Chris five years ago, and we just synced energetically. We went through a roller coaster of hooking up, then not, then potentially being a couple, then just friends. We were never exclusive but still cared for each other. The last time we hooked up was like three years ago, and we were past that attraction. He weirdly became like my brother. He was there for me no matter what. I would even speak to him about my guy problems. He has a girlfriend now, and I'm so happy for him. I don't know if it's just a coincidence or something most girls experience, but I've had some sort of fling in the past with most of my now really close guy friends. We usually end up being friends after we get past the initial attraction.

In my opinion, it would be much harder to stay friends with a guy who I'm even slightly attracted to if it never is explored. I think the difference between an intimate relationship and a friendship is attraction, but once the attraction has passed, you either lose touch or become really good friends. Chris was one of those guys who became a good friend. And it's not like I told Chris I'm not speaking to him anymore; I just slowed the contacts down and then stopped altogether. I thought I was doing it out of respect for my boyfriend. Jay would always drum into my head that guys never just want to be friends; they wanted to sleep with me. Maybe that's true sometimes, but where's the trust on my end? Even if they wanted to, who said I would?

"I'm pissed off with how I sacrificed so much for him. It was so pathetic," I said to Rach, patting my Shitzu cross Maltese puppy under the table.

"Sorry, Scruffy, I don't mean you're pathetic. You're the best," I continued, putting her on my lap. I saw her in the shop window a couple months ago and couldn't let her go. You can give dogs as much love as you want and they will love you back the same. They don't look at you as being weak for loving them. They won't hurt you. A dog's love is pure.

"Well, at least you realize that you're worth more than that now. And that's life; we live and learn. I promise you will evolve from this. And I think being angry with someone who has hurt you is natural but try your hardest to understand someone in that situation ... someone who isn't at peace with themselves. Someone who is unaware of how much they're sabotaging great things in their life. Once you try to understand that, you will have more forgiveness in your heart," she said.

"It's like he doesn't even give a fuck. It's just hard to forgive right now," I answered.

"Yeah, I know, but once you do, you'll be freer. Empathy will take time, but that is the only way to heal. Being empathetic doesn't mean being weak," Rachel insisted.

"Yeah, I guess," I said, taking a bite of my food.

"And it doesn't always mean someone's to blame either, whether they're right or wrong, good or bad. It just means you're on different wavelengths, and that's okay," she continued.

"I know, but I did still love him and felt like we connected. Even though we hadn't known each other for very long, I still feel like it was love."

"And maybe you're right. But we need to allow someone to grow on us, not predetermine the outcome so quickly. Once you start putting in your head 'I want to be with this guy,' especially so early on, it can be very dangerous. I think, if you got to know him better before committing so much, you would've picked up on that. The signs were probably there. That's why you can't completely give yourself so quickly. You need to make sure that the next guy you date is at the maturity level you are," she said.

"Zara and my mom keep saying that it wasn't real love, but I don't usually think about someone so much. I loved hanging out with him. If it wasn't real love, why did I feel like that?" I asked, trying to justify everything I ever felt.

"Well, to be honest, from the outside, it seemed like you started thinking about him more once he started to pull away. At the start, you were cool with him just being there. You were still doing your own thing, and I didn't hear you speak about him as much as you do now," she said.

"Because there's more to talk about now ... he fucked me over."

Rachel got off the chair and started cleaning the kitchen. "How many in-depth conversations did you have with him? How many times was he there for you? How often did he contribute to the relationship when you guys were having an argument? How well did he communicate? Did he fight for you? Did he compromise or understand where you were coming from when you were upset? If he did, you never told me about it. And I know you would've done all those things for him, because you have a beautiful heart. So how could you really love someone who doesn't even have those basic qualities?"

"I've thought about some of those things too. Ahhhh," I moaned after taking a deep breath. "It's just so hard to get him completely out of my system," I said while shaking my body.

"That's it. Shake him off, baby," Rachel said while laughing. "Seriously, though, you gotta work out why you desire certain people so much. I think it's something about you that you have to work on. You deserve a deeper connection. That should be the priority," she added.

I finished my food and put the plate in the sink. I didn't sleep very well last night so I decided to make myself a third coffee.

"I think, because you felt ready for a relationship, you wanted to see him as perfect. I saw you having fun at the start, but for you to tell me that you really liked him after one date shows what you were putting in your mind. Plus, you told me that you felt ready to start seeing someone just weeks before you met him. You were ready to excuse anything he did. How could you know him enough after one night to know you want to be with him? Everyone is on their best behavior when you first meet; they're trying to impress you. That's why you give it time, see how things play out," Rachel said.

"That's not entirely true; I held him off for about a month. He was the one chasing me. He finally got me and then he does this to me," I said.

"Maybe, but I think you forget how invested you were so early on. You might not have shown it to him, but you did to me. I remember telling you to make sure you knew him before you opened your heart," Rachel responded.

"I think that's because I wanted to see the best in him. I like to see the best in people and give them a chance. Maybe I should stop being so open."

"Just don't give your heart away to someone so easily. Share it but never give it away completely. You lose your connection with your soul that way. You need to make sure you're getting what you really want. Remember how we were telling each other what we needed in a guy a while back?"

"Yeah," I responded.

"You gave up a lot of those things when you met Jay. You told me that, for you to be in a serious relationship, he must have strong family values, be self-aware, have direction, and other important stuff.

You wanted someone with a big heart. For one, you wanted that because you were all of those things, and two, you were clear about that because you had dated enough guys to know exactly what you *didn't* want. All those past experiences made what you needed in a partner clearer," Rachel said.

I had honestly forgotten what I'd said I needed in a man. I've always said that you should be with someone who has the same morals and values as you. I don't know how I let that slip from my mind so much.

"I don't know what changed. I had gotten to a stage where I built a lot of those qualities in myself. I thought I didn't need them from anyone else and that I could help them. I thought I was in control of myself… and that no one could really affect that. I was wrong," I said.

As Rachel nodded in agreement, a knock sounded at the door.

CHAPTER 10

MAN

"Who is it?" Rachel called out.

"It's Paul."

Rachel went to the door to let him in. He adores Rachel and has his shit together. He owns a really popular cocktail bar called Mr. Collins. He chased Rachel for so long that she finally gave him a shot. Paul hasn't always been successful, though. When he and Rachel first went out, he wasn't doing very well financially, but he knew what he wanted. He always told Rachel about his visions with the bar and she believed in him. They have stuck by each other so much.

"Can you go down to the shop and get some milk?" Rachel asked him while he was still standing outside the door.

Paul looked at her weirdly and said, "I just bought you milk yesterday. You drank it all?"

Rachel gave him a look, letting him know we were having a serious conversation.

"Ah yeah, cool, I'll be back in a bit. Hey Amelia," he called out, looking over Rachel's shoulder.

"You don't have to go, Paul. You can come in. Rach, it's fine. He knows what's going on," I said.

Paul came into the kitchen. "So how you feeling?" he asked.

"Well, you left the toilet seat up the other day, so not the best."

"Shit, did I? Sorry. I must have been half asleep."

"It's all good. I'm only joking," I said.

Paul went to the fridge and didn't see much in there. "Do you girls not eat or something?"

"I haven't cooked in a while. I really need to start again. Uber Eats has been my best friend. It's sending me broke, though," I said. "I did actually take some initiative the other day. I went to the supermarket to buy fruit and some other stuff. And when I went to buy deodorant, I walked past the condom shelf. Do you know what I thought of?" I asked.

"You felt like sex?" Rachel joked.

"No. Well, it has been a little while. I thought about *him* having sex with another girl," I answered.

Paul burst out laughing. "Yeah, it's crazy how our minds react to this stuff."

"It's ridiculous. I'm relating insignificant things to it, and it's like everyone else's relationship is a reflection of what my life isn't. I heard this song the other day called 'Rise.' It was about some nation rising above the system. And all I could think of was rising above my feelings to get control back," I said.

Paul sat down at the table and faced me. "You know how we hung out a few times, all together? I didn't feel Jay was a man yet. And you're very mature for your age. You need someone on the same level," he said.

"He wasn't like some of the other immature guys I've been with, though," I answered.

"Just like women know other women, guys know other guys. And they know which ones are still boys and which are men. Your judgment was probably clouded," he continued.

"Well, what is a man from a guy's perspective?" I asked.

Paul answered, "To me, a man is over the bullshit. He doesn't make a commitment unless he knows he is ready and then he is mature in the way he goes about it. He understands others because he understands himself. He can rationalize his experiences and choices. He knows his own faults and doesn't always try to blame others for his mistakes. He has goals. He's driven. He has direction. He supports and protects those he loves. And I'm not saying that guys who don't have these qualities yet are bad or those who don't want a relationship aren't men. But if a man is committing to a relationship, he should know what it involves before he does. And I saw how much you liked him, so if he was a man who was ready, that's something he would want to keep. A boy wants to be with girls who are always 'hard to get.' Wise men choose women. They notice beautiful qualities. They're the women they see as being the mother of their children one day—"

"Oh thanks, babe," Rachel interrupted, touching his shoulder.

"You're still working on those, baby," he joked as he touched her hand.

"Oh really? Well, someone isn't getting any tonight," she said, raising her eyebrows and hitting him.

Paul stood up, kissed Rach on the cheek, and held her. He said, "You know I'd die for you—"

"Okay, you guys can seriously stop now," I jokingly interrupted.

"But yeah, anyway, when I met Jay, I just didn't feel that he 'got it,'" he continued saying to me.

"Got what?" I replied.

"It's hard to explain. My friends and I call it 'switched on.' He wasn't switched on in my opinion. He wasn't aware of his surroundings and was still quite ignorant about a lot of important things. I don't think he was that emotionally intelligent either, and I know you are. That makes it very hard to compromise. I've made the mistake of dating girls who don't have that ability, and trust me, it was a fucking nightmare," he answered.

"Honestly, I've questioned whether it never working out is my karma for rejecting great guys in my past," I replied.

"Don't be silly. We all go through it. It just wasn't your time yet. Rachel knows about my ex—"

"Mmm, yeah ... her," Rachel interrupted.

Paul continued, saying, "She made out she was ready, but the signs were there that she wasn't. She was very unsettled within herself and where she was going. She had all these failed relationships and always seemed to blame the guy. She even left a guy just before their wedding. She said that she didn't really love him, but I realized later that wasn't the only issue. I should have picked up on all these things, but I didn't. I ignored a lot.

"She didn't know commitment, and I think she was scared of it to a degree. She didn't understand herself, which didn't allow her to understand others. I ignored the red flags. And look, no one's perfect, but some were big red flags, especially for what I needed in my life. I like more stability and less drama. I guess you just gotta find someone on the same wavelength, who wants to head in the same direction. There's a lot more to it than just attraction, but we all get way too caught up on that," he said.

"Yeah, I get you. Sometimes it's just confusing to know what someone wants, especially when they keep contacting here and there," I said as we moved into the lounge and settled on the sofa.

Paul said, "Look, Amelia, I know you've probably gotten a lot of advice, but I'm going to be upfront. If a guy really wants to be with someone, he will do everything he can, and it will be very clear to you. If he's only coming around here and there, it means he doesn't really want it or is confused. And on the odd occasion that he does want it and isn't being clear, then he's not a man. He should man up and grow some balls, and if he won't, then you don't want that. He misses out. That's it. Also, if I were you, I wouldn't be making myself available for his every call. He lost that privilege."

Rach jumped in and said, "Like they say, out of sight, out of mind. It will take a while for him to leave your mind, but you're just delaying it by still following him on Insta and keeping in touch. Block him. It doesn't matter what he thinks. It's about you now."

"I honestly just feel like I'm never going to find someone. I don't know what the difference is between me and other girls who are in happy relationships," I said, remembering all the times it hasn't worked out.

"We've all been infatuated with someone who isn't right for us. Even my guy friends go through it. Your intelligence just needs to override your emotions, and that will take time," Paul replied. "My dad said to me before he passed, 'Son, follow your heart, but take your brain with you.' I use that in every part of my life and it's helped me a lot. And don't stress; you will choose the right person when you are ready. You just have to stop falling for people so quickly. You need to be more aware."

"I'll be all right. It just feels like shit being rejected. Anyway, thanks for the chats. Love you two," I said, getting off the couch.

"We're gonna watch a movie. Want to join?" Rachel asked.

"No, it's okay. You guys go ahead. I'm going to try to get some sleep," I replied, walking to my room. "Oh, by the way, Zara wants me to go to New York with her in a few weeks," I continued.

"Be careful. You know I love Zara but don't do anything over there you'll regret," Rachel replied.

June 29, 2019, at 12:26 a.m.

This constant dating game is really wasting people's lives. Think about how much energy is spent on it, how many thoughts we have about other people in regard to dating.it's ridiculous and driving us all nuts. Like seriously, what is going on? We're happy, sad, anxious, nervous,angry, excited, agitated, and that's in a single week. My energy needs to better spent, but I keep coming around to this point. WHY?

Some people say, "wish him the best." He screwed me over. I'm not gonna pretend like I want the best for him right now,because I don't.

I need to learn to adapt quicker. Plans fall through, things change, people change, sometimes in an instant. I have to learn accept it

-get food and new bowl for Scruffy.

lust is so fucking bad. It's so dangerous it can destroy your life if not carefully acknowledged, then corrected.

Remember, you can't force a connection.

We are dating and meeting so many different people these days, it's like our relationships are in short bursts. They aren't fulfilling. They aren't given enough time. They just take our energy, our self-worth.

I need to remember that if they message out of the blue,not to get fooled. It doesn't mean they want to be with me, it might mean they are bored or just thought about me in that moment

-start reading that self-help book Rachel gave me. Pay phone and energy bill.

July 7, 2019, at 1:12 p.m.

Harder to please people these days.

I want to feel an undeniable love for myself again

Sometimes in life you meet someone who you connect with so much, you want to them to stay in your life forever . . . even if it's just as friends. It's that unexplained sync of two souls.

We face so much rejection, it's making us all self-conscious. Then we reject those who treat us well because we are insecure,which makes them insecure. I really want to get off that wheel and find more depth in my life. Something more real.

Even when I can't see the light at the end of the tunnel, I still be-lieve it's there

everyone's seeking perfection in someone these days . . . that's the fucking problem.i'm not perfect, okay? I'm sorry. .

CHAPTER 11

GROWTH

Rachel

I was someone who expected things from people I knew weren't mature enough to give them to me. I pursued them anyway. I had forgotten who I was and what I deserved. I thought my happiness was solely dependent on the way others treated me, how they looked at me, what they thought about me, or how much attention they gave me. I would always call my guy cousin and talk to him about dating. I would tell him the guys I liked needed to grow up and be straight with me. One day he said to me very bluntly, "Rach, the truth is that you're the one who needs to grow up and stop wanting guys who keep fucking you around." It was so true. I had to take responsibility for my own life. I kept chasing guys who I knew in my heart weren't ever going to commit or give me what I needed. Sometimes I became so fixated on trying to catch someone, I lost sight of everything else in my life. They'd call me "baby" or ask things like "have you been with anyone else?" but they'd never commit to me. It was all a lie. I tried to hold on to them for as long as I could, but in the process, I slipped farther away from who I was.

I had to be smarter when picking a partner. I needed someone who hung around longer than a few weeks, someone who didn't only want to see me when it suited them. Some of the good guys were right in front of my face. I didn't give them enough of a chance or allow them to grow on me because I assumed they wouldn't make me happy. I thought I needed a guy who challenged me from the start.

I've been with Paul for three years now, and my girls think he's going to propose soon. He's been dropping hints apparently. When I first met him, I was over dating. I had been screwed around so many times by guys I thought I needed in my life. But Paul was nice to me and present. He would text me often and showed interest, and I must admit it turned me off a bit. But eventually, I let him take me out. It wasn't as explosive in the beginning as other guys, but he charmed me over time because I became open to him. He was so much funnier than what I initially thought. I gave myself the opportunity to get to know him and not assume so quickly. And not assuming anymore didn't mean I was ignoring red flags...oh no, quite the opposite. This time I went in with more awareness (and maybe a touch of fear). I had to make sure he was the real deal.

In my past, when I was really physically attracted to someone, I would automatically assume they would be good for me. I had to fight through that mind-set when I realized what I'd been doing because it only brought me pain. I needed to give guys who were really interested in me a chance. And I can tell you now, Paul isn't the pushover I thought he might be. He's strong but kind. At the start, he took my shit a lot. As with most relationships, we got more comfortable and the energy balanced out. Now he puts me in my place when I'm giving him shit. He doesn't just take it...I like that. And

I do the same with him. We challenge, motivate, and support each other. My point is that, if I never got past wanting someone who didn't want me and actually gave other people a chance, I would've continued assuming they weren't right for me and missed out on something amazing.

I'm not naive; I don't think Paul is perfect or mistake-proof. I'm not saying he doesn't affect the way I feel sometimes, but I haven't put all of myself into him. I'm still my own person and have my own life, and he understands that. I wouldn't say I'm crazy in love...I'm genuinely in love. Paul and I are rocky sometimes, but I know he is worth it because I got to know his heart. A life partner helps brings out the best in you; they don't take advantage of your weaknesses.

Unlike Jay. In my opinion, he never really committed to Amelia. When you become intertwined in each other's lives, each other's problems, and each other's growth, it can be a different story to the honeymoon phase. And as we know in life, there can be some hard times. I think you can tell more about a person's character by how they act when things aren't going well. It's easy to stick around when things are great, but commitment and loyalty are truly tested during hardship.

I really want Amelia to rebuild the beautiful relationship she once had with herself. She saw herself in such a beautiful light. But you know, things happen to make us wiser and build an even stronger bond with our soul. This experience will help her evolve if she faces the truth and allows the proper thoughts to come through. The problem is, she tries to evolve the people she likes and help them see what she sees. That's a beautiful trait but not when she's losing herself in the process.

You can't force someone to evolve with you. It either happens naturally with effort from both sides, or it doesn't happen at all. That's what it was like with her and Jay, I think. She was expecting him to see things the way she did, but she had come really far in understanding herself. I think he was at a crossroads in his life when she met him; he didn't know what he wanted. She thought she could help him make that clearer. And maybe she did, just not the way she wanted.

CHAPTER 12

SHE'S READ IT

Five weeks later—New York vacation ... *continued*

Nick (that guy from the bar)

"I'm happy to be back here," I said to Jordan as the condo door closed behind us.

It's been a while since Jordan and I spent time together here in New York. We grew up here together, but the past couple of years, I've been traveling for work. We decided to book a really nice place downtown. I love the meatpacking district. I think I've eaten a panini from that Italian deli at Chelsea Market every day.

Jordan grabbed a beer out of the fridge and walked over to the sofa in the main room. "Do you think the girls will come? They didn't look like they wanted to leave," he said as he sat down.

"I messaged Amelia the address about forty-five minutes ago. She's read it but hasn't replied yet," I answered.

"Don't text again. We'll look too desperate," he replied.

I laughed at him. "I want to know what's going on. And why do you care so much about how we'll look? They're the ones who said they'd come. If they don't, we'll make other plans."

If I had a dollar for every time Jordan was too nice to people and got screwed, I'd have a lot more money. He also lets them affect his emotions way too often. He fears losing people he's interested in, even those he hardly knows. That fear of loss holds him back from saying what he really wants. You know that "walking on thin ice" feeling? You gotta find that perfect balance of showing interest without being too interested. Too much weight on one side and you sink. I just feel like he's in that zone way too often. He always asks me questions like, "Why do they act interested and then not follow through? Why do they text and then not respond when I try to meet up? Why do they bail on dates?" It's like he has learned nothing from all the experiences he's had. He keeps coming back to the same point, asking the same questions.

I don't understand how he's still surprised when it's so common. He needs to grasp that most people are just doing their own thing and have certain priorities. The truth is, he isn't a priority to certain people. And I guess, in this day and age, most people are fucked. It's what suits them at that moment. They lack common decency. They're selfish. If it doesn't suit them to write back, they won't. The truth is, some people play games and are just really fucking rude. They've got no integrity and their word means nothing.

Don't get me wrong. I know the game needs to be played on occasions, especially with some people who are used to getting a lot of attention, but I honestly don't have the patience for it anymore. Who the fuck does? I played back and forth with people for years. Now, I act like myself more times than not, and I think it challenges people more than anything. When you give less fucks about trying to be something you're not, people are drawn to you. Everyone wishes they could be themselves unapologetically. In the past, if I really liked someone or was infatuated, I'd try to get on their level just so they'd like me back. I pretended to like what they liked or agreed with them even though, deep down, I might have had a different view. But I don't do that anymore.

You know, it's funny. The less I care about what people think of me, the more power I find—not just within myself but with others too. People can feel your strength, and sometimes they want you to be weaker than they are. There's a quote that says, "The one who cares less holds more power." But I don't think it's about caring less than the other person; it's about staying who you are and not losing yourself just to please someone else.

I understand how it works now. I understand that people have their own insecurities. I understand that the lack of respect someone has for others is a reflection of the respect they have for themselves. Also, I don't date as often as I used to. I don't spend 80 percent of my time thinking about it. It's more like 20 percent now. The other 80 is used to enjoy my life and get ahead in my career, travel, experience new things. I stopped living a life where I only reacted to the way others treated me. If someone wants to be in my life, they will be. If not, I'm not going to keep chasing.

"I just messaged Amelia again," I said, sitting down on the sofa.

"What did you say?"

I wrote to her, "Hey, if you girls can't make it, all good. We're gonna make other plans. It was really nice meeting you, though. Maybe we'll bump into each other in the future. Take care, smiley face."

Not even five minutes went by and my phone vibrated in my pocket. It was Amelia. She wrote, "Hey, I'm sorry, we got caught up. We can be there in about half an hour. That okay?"

"Yeah, cool," I replied.

I grabbed the whiskey off the coffee table in front of me, pulled the cork top, and poured about a quarter up. I'm not a big drinker, but sometimes I love a good whiskey. Something with layers and depth. The older I'm getting, the smoother I need it.

"She just wrote back and said they're coming soon," I said to Jordan.

"That quick?" he asked.

"Yeah, I guess you gotta be to the point sometimes. If it works, it works. If not, you have your answer," I said.

"Yeah, but easier said than done. Oh, forgot to tell you—remember Nicole, the girl I met at Justin's party last year?"

"Yeah. What about her?"

"She won't speak to me anymore and is telling people I fucked her around."

"Did you?" I asked.

"I didn't think so. We were only having sex, but I still liked her as a person. Just because I didn't want a relationship doesn't mean I don't care about her," Jordan said in his semi-drunken state.

"Maybe you gave her mixed messages. We can keep sleeping with a girl and not think more of it. A lot of girls aren't like that," I said.

"Mixed messages? She would literally come over and have sex and that's it. We never went out and did anything. We used to chat and hang when she was here, but there wasn't more to it. Sometimes we didn't see each other for a month. I never said anything to her that would make her believe there *could* be more," Jordan replied.

"Did you ever say you missed her or anything like that? Did she stay the night?" I asked.

"Yeah, she slept over a lot of nights. And sometimes I said I missed her but only because I genuinely did."

"You can't say those things, especially if you only have the intention of seeing her sometimes."

I know that Jordan probably gave mixed messages without meaning to hurt her or give the wrong impression, of course. He did like Nicole. I know that.

Jordan sat down on the chair across from me with his beer and said, "Honestly, man, I thought she was cool to keep it how it was. I'm not dumb. I thought she might have feelings, but she never said anything to me about it. We both just went with it.... It's a shame how she's just fuckin' turned on me.

"I just don't want a relationship with anyone right now. I've got too much shit going on. I don't think they understand that we can love being intimate without wanting an actual relationship. She probably thinks I don't respect her, but I do. It's got nothing to do with that," he continued.

"Maybe you should've told her you didn't want anything more."

"I've done that in the past and the girl got all pissed off and was like, "I didn't want anything more either," he said. "Anyway, girls are just as much players these days."

"What happened now?"

"I got this girl's number from Tinder and we've been chatting a fair bit. I've spoken to her on the phone a few times too. She texted me last Saturday night saying, 'Hey babe, what are you up to tonight? Want to maybe grab a drink?' Justin was at my place and I showed him what she looked like. He told me he matched with her a few days before. And that's cool; everyone is matching everyone. But two minutes after she messaged me, she messaged him the exact same thing. God knows how many others. And while we're on the Tinder subject, have you seen some of their pictures and bios? I don't get it," Jordan said.

"What about 'em? You know I haven't had Tinder in years," I replied.

"Me and the boys were baffled going through it the other night. Some of these girls put up photos with their tongue out between their fingers, crouching down with their hand on their pussy at a festival, both hands up against a wall bending over and sticking their ass out...and then their bio is, 'Looking for a real man' or 'No hookups. Gentlemen only need apply.' No gentleman is going to take them seriously when they give off that first impression," Jordan continued.

"They'd eat you alive if you said that to them. And give 'em a break, man. They're probably just young girls," I said.

"Well, Jacqui was at my place last week and asked if she could swipe my Tinder. Even she was shocked with some of their profiles. And that's the thing; they're not all young. Some of them were like twenty-eight or twenty-nine. And I'm just being realistic, man.

"Oh, and don't worry, girls judge guys just as much. Jacqui was saying that, if she sees a profile of a guy with his top off, especially a bathroom selfie, she swipes left instantly," he said.

Jacqui is one of our best friends. We all went to school together.

"I actually started liking that girl from Tinder, the one that hit up Justin on the same night. Guess I can't take her seriously anymore," Jordan continued.

"Girls know what we're up to ... so if it's good for us, it's good for them too," I said.

"I'm not saying it's not. Everyone is having sex with everyone these days. But so many of them make out like we're the only guys they're talking to. They think we're stupid. Then they use that 'player' shit on us. We're always the 'bad' ones. They're going on dates with different guys all the time, and who knows how many they speak to with Tinder and shit. Then they get pissed off when they find out we're chatting to other girls. So, it's okay for them to do trial and error but not for us. Guys talk now, so that innocent card doesn't work anymore. We know what's going on," he continued.

"Yeah, but I think we usually catch up with a lot of girls because we want sex. They go on dates with different guys to see if they can potentially *be* with them," I said.

"Come on, we get fucked over by girls we like all the time. They just don't know it because we don't express it as much. Honestly, that's why it's better to give less," he continued.

"What do you mean?"

"I always hear girls asking where all the really nice guys have gone or where all the men have gone. But I want to know where all the women have gone. And that nice- guy thing is bullshit. Most girls are just focusing on the guys who don't give a fuck about 'em. The guy who would take a bullet for 'em isn't noticed," he said, standing up and walking around the room. "And just because we're nice to certain ones, it doesn't mean we're like that with every girl. But it doesn't make them feel special anymore. They take it as being desperate. Do you know what's weird too?"

"What?" I replied, having a drink of my whiskey.

"A lot of times, when you take them out for dinner on the first date or do something really sweet, nothing ever comes of it. But when you invite them over and sleep with them right away, they're into you instantly. I don't get it. Seems like not being fully into them is more rewarding. If you're too nice, you're out the door. In reality, they don't appreciate it like they say," he said, going to the fridge and getting another beer.

"We do it too, though. We have beautiful girls who like us, but then we chase the girl who plays hard to get," I said.

"You know more than anyone that most guys are in a battle when they start to like a girl ... either be open and really nice or stay a bit more closed and in control," he said.

"The gap is closing between men and women, and you gotta learn to accept that," I said.

"What I'm saying has nothing to do with that. I have accepted it. And just because I understand men sometimes too, does that mean I'm against feminism or that I don't respect women? No, I'm sorry, but that's absolute bullshit! There are both sexes in all of this and we both need to be understood. It doesn't only go one way, man. I was raised by women, so don't go making out like I don't respect them," Jordan said. "But we as guys have views too. We don't like everything that's going on out there either. We say one word about a person (who happens to be a woman sometimes) and we get crucified, so we don't say it. We keep it in, think what we think, and it affects the way we act. They can say whatever they like to us or about us, and it's fine. If they want to understand us more, then they have to listen and stop being so ready to attack," he continued.

"Yeah, go on," I replied, listening to his rant.

"I think girls have to be honest with themselves about what they want. If it's a guy who isn't going to give her much, then she has to admit that and stop pretending she wants something else. Because I can assure you, a lot of times, when that guy comes along who gives her a lot, she doesn't accept it. Maybe that's where the truth is. Maybe that's when they're more comfortable in the situation...when they come to terms with what they really want in a guy, not what kind of guy they pretend to want," he said.

"Yeah, but everyone is looking for different things. So, I guess it's up to the individual girl what she really wants," I answered.

"That's my point. But don't constantly say you want something and then, when it comes along, push it away. I think the truth is, half of them don't know what the fuck they want. So how are we meant to know what they want?" Jordan added passionately.

I did see what Jordan was saying and have experienced it many times. But I guess that recently I've noticed we equally treat each other like this. We're all to blame for how messy the dating scene is. But yeah, it's been frustrating to me too on many occasions. When I really liked a girl and she became disinterested because I was open too soon, it really pissed me off. And sometimes it happened so often that it made me less open with many girls after that. I didn't want to play games, but when I let my guard down and showed my emotions too quickly, the same thing happened. It was a shame that so many girls took my moments of vulnerability as weakness.

I've also noticed with a lot of guys I know, when they've been deeply hurt by a girl in the past, it takes a long time to be themselves again with another one. It takes years sometimes. And even if they do settle with a girl in the future, a lot of times, they won't be the same as they were with the girl who broke their heart. They think they have to be "stronger" and have a harder shell or they'll lose her.

I believe girls are truly stronger than guys, even though they don't think it sometimes. I've noticed girls will put themselves out there and risk being hurt more often. They're more courageous than we are. For years, I kept telling myself that I didn't want to be with someone because I might hurt them. But I think the truth was that I was the one who was scared to get hurt. It took me a very long time to get over what my ex did to me. Sometimes it still crosses my mind.

CHAPTER 13

GUY TALK

Jordan walked out on the balcony and spoke to me from there. "So many girls assume that they know what we're like. They think we're statues, but we think, we feel, we see what's going on. And yeah, it's true we don't want to date every girl we sleep with, but that doesn't mean we don't fall for girls either. Sometimes there are reasons some guys are closed off."

I poured more whiskey in my glass. "In regard to what? And don't go talking about this shit when the girls come. I don't want to get into arguments. We're on vacation," I said.

"Take it easy, man. I'm not an idiot. I'm not gonna fuck the night up. It's us here; that's why I'm speaking like this."

"Go on then," I insisted.

"What's the incentive to be a gentleman when they don't even appreciate it? Can you imagine taking them a bunch of flowers or a box of chocolates on the first date now? They'd think you're a fucking loser or a creep. Seems like a sweet thought in their head, but in reality, it doesn't work anymore. Message a few times in a row without a reply and you're out the door. We're scared to be ourselves. In so many ways, we aren't allowed to be men. What we really want to do when we like a girl is winning them over less and less, so we don't do it," he added.

"Yeah, I definitely wouldn't be taking a box of chocolates. *You're* likely to do something like that," I joked.

"You get what I mean…stop being a smart-ass. I've spent my whole life being nice to girls and getting fucked around. All the ones who are chasing me are doing it because I don't care. The ones I really want, I give them my attention, and I end up on the back foot. Like honestly, what is going on out there?" he said, leaning on the glass balcony ledge and smoking a cigarette. "Remember that girl I met a few weeks back? The blond one?" he continued.

"I think so. Was she with that other girl who had the green eyes?" I asked.

"Yeah. When I met her that night, she was telling me how much she hates playing games. She said she appreciated gentlemen. A few days later, she messages asking how I am. I replied and asked if she wanted to catch up soon. She said yes and gave me two options: Wednesday or Friday. I told her Friday is better. Friday comes—actually here, I'll show you the messages." Jordan pulled out his phone and opened the message. "On Friday at 12:48 p.m., I sent her this,

> Hey hope you've had a good week. What time are you free tonight?

She responds ten minutes later saying,

> Hey babe, I'll be free after 8 if that suits you? x

I write back and say,

Yeah, that works. How's 8:30 in the city? X ☺.'"

"I probably would've avoided the big kiss and the smile emoji in the last message. She's not putting any emotion in her texts, so you shouldn't. But go on," I said, sort of joking to piss him off. There probably was truth in it, though.

"Oh, come on, man. If she didn't respond because of that, I fucking give up. I did it because I thought my texts were looking boring."

"So, what happened?"

"She didn't respond. I waited until about eight and decided to call. No answer and no call back. Then, around nine, I see her post on Insta that she's out for drinks with her friend. Can you believe that? She messages me, suggests a night, then completely ignores me. Did I say something wrong?" Jordan said in a frustrated tone.

"You did nothing wrong. She could have at least let you know she couldn't make it," I replied.

"See, this is the shit I don't do to people. Honestly, what pathetic excuse for a human being plans a specific time and day with someone and doesn't even have the respect to communicate? That's so fucked," Jordan added.

"I told you about that girl recently that kept texting me?" I asked.

"Yeah," he responded.

"I was driving in the car and thought I'd call because I couldn't be bothered texting. She didn't answer and never responded to my text again. I actually think calling her scared her off. It's a joke. Most people can't even chat other than through text or an app," I said.

"But I must admit, sometimes I can't be fucked speaking on the phone," Jordan said, lighting up a joint. I was happy he decided to have weed. It might mellow him out a bit.

"The problem is, people just don't have respect these days. The dating game has changed. It's not like it used to be. Good gestures are appreciated less and less," he said.

Jordan walked back in and sat down. "I loved my ex, man. I would have jumped in front of a train for her, and now she's with that dickhead who treats her like shit, and she's posting him all over Insta. Tell me about that, Nick. Huh? Where's the justice in that? And it's happening with all these other girls I meet," he said in a softer tone.

"Look, you have a point, but I think a lot of it has to do with you being nice to the wrong ones. That's why they don't appreciate it. You're chasing these immature girls who don't give a fuck about anyone but themselves. You know we don't settle with girls like that. They're not girls we marry. When you're ready, you'll find a girl who deserves it. There are girls out there with a beautiful heart, but you're ignoring them. And then they turn sour because they think they have to act like the other women you chase to attract guys," I said.

"It's a vicious circle, isn't it?" Jordan replied.

I took another sip of my whiskey. "Yes. We all think we have to be closed off to keep someone. But it's not true; that's just trying to keep the wrong people, the people who you can't even be yourself with," I said.

I knew Jordan still hadn't come to terms with why his ex left him. She broke up with him about four months ago, but that's still pretty recent considering he loved her to death. He treated her like a princess, and what she said when they broke up was, "I love you; I'm just not *in love* with you anymore." I never bought that. I think she just got bored. And like a child bored of their toy, she threw it away because she wanted a new one. But the signs were always there that she wasn't right for Jordan. All she seemed to care about was herself and impressing people over social media. She was shallow, but he held on for some reason.

"I guess you're right. I think it's some fucked-up mind game because I feel like I lost so much power with my ex. Maybe I feel like these new girls I meet are my ex in a way. I want that power to make myself feel better. I want them to like me the way I wanted my ex to like me," he said.

"Yeah, it's psychological," I added.

Jordan walked back inside, saying, "It's always fake satisfaction, though. I've gotta break this cycle and make changes. It's not good for my sanity."

"I'll never marry a girl who is surface and too caught up in fake bullshit. I need depth and substance. I need a woman who's real," I said.

"You know what, man? I want to stop holding on to resentment toward my ex. I really do. People are looking for different things at different stages of their life. Doesn't mean they're bad people, just different. Look now, she's into her new boyfriend the way I wanted her to be into me. I have to accept that not everyone is for me, and I'm not for everyone," Jordan said wisely.

"Exactly. That's one of the hardest things, but when you do, you'll grow in life, especially with someone you could really connect with. You'll settle with a beautiful woman who loves you one day. You're a good guy; you deserve it," I said to Jordan.

"You should be a counselor. You're good at this shit," Jordan said, laughing.

"Go fuck yourself," I jokingly replied.

CHAPTER 14

THEY COMING?

Thirty-seven minutes later . . .

"I don't think they're coming. We can always message those other girls we met," Jordan suggested.

"No, Zara and Amelia were nicer. They'll come."

"Did you see Zara's ass in that dress? Fuckin' hell."

"Yeah, it was sexy, but I don't know. I wanted Amelia more," I replied.

"You liked her hands and feet too, didn't you? I've known you for too long," Jordan replied.

"You know I like when they look after their nails. But she didn't overdo it either. It was like she didn't care that she wasn't tanned or didn't have much makeup on. I liked that. She looked after herself in a subtle way. She had a softer nature too," I said.

At the bar, I'd spoken to Zara more because I ended up physically closer to her, but I couldn't stop looking at Amelia. I wanted her as soon as I saw her. There was something about her. She just seemed cool, easygoing, no bullshit. Zara probably gets a lot more attention than she does, but it's not about being the most dolled-up girl for me. I just liked Amelia's energy more.

Nine minutes later . . .

My phone vibrated in my pocket. It was Amelia calling.

"Hey," I answered.

"Hey, sorry we're late. The Uber driver took the longest way. Anyway, we're downstairs."

"Okay, cool. I'll call reception and get someone to walk you up."

"Hey!" I screamed out to Jordan. He was upstairs.

"Yeah?"

"The girls are here. They'll be up in a minute."

I rang reception then quickly went to the bathroom to make sure I was still looking human. I'd been slouching on the couch for the past two hours. I brushed my teeth and sprayed some cologne on my neck just as the knock on the door sounded.

"Hey, how are you?" Zara asked as I opened the door.

"Great!" I answered, kissing her hello on the cheek.

When I saw Amelia, we stared into each other's eyes.

"Hey," I said, while putting my hand lightly on her waist and kissing her hello. Our lips almost touched. I felt like we both did it intentionally.

"Wow, this place is amazing," Zara said.

"Yeah, we love it. It's actually better than the pictures. Make yourselves at home. Do you girls want a drink?"

Zara walked over to the lounge and put down her jacket and clutch. She held on to her phone, though.

"Sure. What do you have?" she asked.

"I put some champagne in the fridge earlier today, so that's cold, or we have vodka."

"Champagne sounds nice," Amelia said, slurring her words a little. She was a bit more drunk than she was at the bar.

"Is it cool to have a smoke on the balcony?" Zara asked.

"Yeah. There's another one upstairs if you want to check out the other level. Jordan will probably have one with you. He's up there."

"Do you want one, Nick? Amelia?" Zara asked us.

"No, thank you. I'm good for now," I replied.

"I'll help Nick with the drinks," Amelia answered straight after me.

Zara walked upstairs while Amelia followed me to the kitchen.

"So, how was the bar when we left?" I asked.

"It got crazy. Seriously, I haven't been to New York in so long. It was fun, but then these drunk guys wouldn't leave us alone. They ended up getting kicked out by security," Amelia said, nervously looking away when she was talking. I think we were both still thinking about our kiss hello at the front door.

"Yeah, that's why we left. It was getting a bit out of hand in there," I said, my back to her while I was getting the champagne glasses from the top shelf.

There was silence while I poured the drinks. Neither of us spoke. I wanted her closer to me again, but her shyness made me question how to go about it.

I turned around and passed her a glass of champagne.

"Thank you," she said, having a sip and then putting it down on the counter.

We just stared at each other, silently, thinking the same thing. I put my hand out and slowly pulled her closer to me.

"You're so beautiful," I said as she was closer to my face.

"Really? I honestly didn't think I'd be your type," she replied, looking down.

I put my hand under her chin and lifted her face until we locked eyes. I could feel her warm breath against my lips. I started kissing her, biting her bottom lip softly. She started biting mine back. The way she kissed me, it was like she was a different person. Her shyness just seemed to go.

I soon moved down to her neck, kissing it and using my tongue. With one hand on her head and the other on the back of her neck, I held her more tightly. Slowly, we started rubbing up against each other. The more intense it got, the harder I got. She was making me so horny. I wanted to lift her up on the kitchen counter, wrap her legs around my waist, and push deep inside her.

We heard Jordan and Zara laughing as they were coming down the stairs. *Can you believe the fucking timing?*

Amelia quickly fixed herself. I wiped my lips and turned back around to get the drinks.

"Where's the champagne? You guys still haven't poured all of them?" Zara said.

"Where's your bathroom?" Amelia asked.

Jordan showed her where it was. Zara followed her in there.

"What the fuck did you do to her?" Jordan whispered to me.

"Nothing. Why?" I asked.

"Because she looked rattled and quickly went to the bathroom. I think they're gonna leave."

"Chill the fuck out. We just kissed and you guys came down. She freaked out a bit. They're just having girl talk," I said.

CHAPTER 15

THE BATHROOM

Amelia

"You should see upstairs. This place is huge," Zara said as she locked the bathroom door behind us.

"We just hooked up," I said, flustered.

"You and Nick?"

"No, me and the statue."

"That was quick. We just got here. And what's wrong? He's hot," Zara replied, fixing her dress in the mirror.

I sat on the toilet and started peeing. "I just freaked out a bit, but it was so hot. He actually knows how to kiss me ... with passion but not crazy.

He made me wet and we hardly did anything. I think I want to sleep with him tonight."

"Do what you want, but don't call me regretting it later. Anyway, if I were you, though, I probably would. Six weeks... I don't know how you've survived," Zara replied.

I finished on the toilet and faced the mirror. My eyes were bloodshot from the alcohol. "I think I'm ready. He's the only guy I've wanted to do it with since Jay. The way he just held me... I haven't been held like that for so long. I know it might just be for the moment, but it felt so good," I replied, remembering how good he smelled too. I could still smell his cologne on my top.

"What were you and Jordan talking about? You seemed to be getting along," I asked.

"He's a really funny guy. And he seems a bit innocent. I think I'm gonna have fun with him tonight... I might show him a few things," Zara replied, fixing her makeup.

"Oh, did you see the champagne Nick got out?" I asked.

"No. What was it?"

"It was Veuve. It's what I was going to drink with Jay on my birthday. You gave me the bottles, remember?"

"Yeah. What's your point?"

"I don't know. Weird shit just happens to me like that. It's like everything is connected. And for the past few days, I keep seeing eleven-eleven and one-eleven," I said.

"Amelia, don't look into stuff too hard."

"I'm not. Recently, everything has just felt out of place. For the first time in a while, I feel like I'm exactly where I'm meant to be," I answered.

"Are you cool to go back out?" Zara asked.

"Yeah," I said, taking a deep breath and composing myself.

CHAPTER 16

GOING WITH THE FLOW

Nick

"Are you girls okay?" I said as they came out of the bathroom.

"Yeah, we're fine," Amelia responded.

I gave the girls their drinks and put some music on. We all sat in the lounge for the next hour, drinking and talking shit. Zara and Jordan were getting closer.

"What music are you into?" I asked Amelia.

"Honestly, people would probably think I'm a weirdo if they saw my playlists. I literally listen to every kind of music depending on my mood," she answered.

"Let's see what you've got," I said, passing her my phone.

"Umm, how's some Billie Eilish? I've had her on repeat for the past three weeks, I think. I'm actually obsessed," she answered.

Zara quickly interrupted, "Not at this time on a Saturday night, Amelia."

"Okay, okay, let me see. What about this? Not sure if you're into house."

She played the classic "Electricity" by Lee Foss and MK feat Anabel.

"Great track!" Jordan called out. He got Zara up and started jokingly dancing, singing the vocals to her as well. He was making her laugh...a lot.

"I first heard this song on my trip to Mykonos a few years ago," I said to Amelia.

"Really? I heard it on my first trip to Europe last year. They played it on my boat when I did 'Sail Croatia.' This track takes me back to that boat so much. I felt so free," she replied.

She was lying down on the couch, her head resting on my lap. I looked down at her and said, "I still haven't shown you the place properly. Do you want a tour?"

"Sure," she said, smirking. I'm guessing she knew what I had in mind.

"I'm gonna show Amelia the place," I said to Zara and Jordan. They didn't even hear me; they were in their own world by this stage.

I held her hand while she followed me up the stairs. I was treading carefully with her for some reason. We probably would've already had sex by now if it was someone else. A drunken 2:00 a.m. catch-up usually leads to things pretty quickly. But Amelia made me slightly nervous. I don't think she picked up on it, though.

"Wow, there are exercise machines?" she said, walking over to the bicycles overlooking the city.

I held her from behind as we both looked out at New York. I soon moved her hair away from her neck and started kissing it slowly. Using my tongue and breathing warm air on her ear, she put her hand near my groin and started rubbing it. She slowly increased the pressure and soon I couldn't handle it anymore. I quickly walked her over to my room, turned on the lamp, and shut the door. Kissing her against the wall, I pulled down her top from her left shoulder and sucked on her nipple, using my teeth softly.

"Bite it a bit harder," she whispered.

She started moaning. I took my shirt off, lifted her skirt up above her waist, got down my knees, and put her leg over my shoulder. I started running the tip of my tongue along the inside of her leg. She was rubbing my back and scratching it lightly. I teased her, moving my mouth slowly over her pussy, kissing it softly, then moving to her other leg. I looked up at her; she looked down in my eyes. I put my tongue on her clit then two fingers inside her. She moaned more, her head falling back against the wall. I was so fucking hard hearing her moan. I grabbed her hand and put it on the back of my head, pushing my mouth more firmly onto her pussy. She pushed it in harder, my tongue and fingers moving faster.

"Keep going... I'm about to come," she whispered.

Already? I thought.

"*Oh my God. What the fuck is that?!*" she yelled, quickly pushing me away and pulling her skirt down.

"What? What's the matter?" I said, confused.

"*That*," she replied, pointing at my camera and video recorder. "Are you fucking recording this?"

"Oh my God, Amelia, it's off. I told you I like photography. Go over and see," I insisted.

She walked over to the camera. "Shit, it *is* off. I'm so sorry. I'm not ready for all of this ... I thought I was," she said, sitting on the bed and rubbing her forehead. "You must hate me."

"I don't hate you. But I don't really know what to think either. One minute you're about to come; the next you're saying you're not ready," I replied.

Of course, I was frustrated and a little pissed. But what was I supposed to say? She was too sweet. I couldn't be angry with her. Instead, I started feeling sorry for her. But geez, my dick was about to explode.

"What's up? Obviously, something is messing with your head. A guy?" I asked.

"Yeah, it's my ex, but it's also my experience with guys in general. I shouldn't even be speaking to you about this ... we just nearly had sex. I feel like a bitch," she said.

"It's all good. I'm not taking offense. You obviously want to talk about it?" I asked.

CHAPTER 17

THE CONVERSATION

Amelia

"I don't know. I just think there's just too much miscommunication between guys and girls. I mean, no one knows what the fuck is going on. We need to have the discussion. We need to vent it and get it out in the open," I said, grabbing my drink from the bedside table.

Nick sat on the edge of the bed and put his shirt back on. "What do you want to know?"

"I just want to know what guys are thinking. I mean we have sex and stuff, and nothing lasting ever comes of it," I said, taking a cigarette out of the packet next to his bed and lighting it. I knew

I shouldn't be smoking in the room, but I was too drunk to care. "I'm not usually a smoker, by the way."

"Me neither. I might have one here and there on a holiday, but that's it. They're one of Jordan's packs," he replied. "And when it comes to what guys are thinking, I don't think I should say. We don't know everything girls are thinking. Some things are better left unsaid."

"I want to know. I'd prefer shit to be clearer, because I'm always confused," I said. I could tell he was still a bit sexually frustrated, but he seemed okay to chat.

"Go ahead then, ask what you want. I'll try give it to you as straight as I can. But don't hate the messenger," Nick responded, taking the champagne from my hand and having some.

"I won't, promise. So why do guys act so interested and then not get in touch at all?" I asked.

"Do you mean guys you've been with for a while or guys you just met?" he asked.

"Both. I'm confused with both."

"Well, I can't really comment on a guy you've been with for a while because I don't know what happened between you. But I will say that, when I wasn't ready for a relationship, even with girls I was seeing, nothing was good enough. But I didn't want anything more with anyone. I met beautiful girls, inside and out, but it still wasn't enough. Nothing was. That's why when they say, 'Nothing's ever good enough for that person,' maybe it's true," Nick replied. "And sometimes if they're really fucked up, they end up with someone who doesn't treat them as good as you. That comes from pain in his past. And I would stay clear of even thinking about those guys," he continued.

"And what about, generally speaking, guys I just meet? I never know what their true intentions are. Do they just want to fuck me? I was seeing this guy before my ex, Jay, and we slept together regularly and would hang out sometimes. I really liked him, but he never pursued anything," I said.

He replied, "I think it was just convenient for him to keep sleeping with you on his terms. It doesn't mean a guy doesn't like or respect you if he's sleeping with you, but I doubt he will want more if he hasn't pursued it yet. If a guy's been seeing you a lot and is serious about it, he'll involve you in his life. He'll invite you to things he gets invited to; he will take you to family gatherings to meet everyone—"

"Yeah, I guess," I interrupted.

"And if you've been seeing him for a while, ask him what's happening between you two. You will get your answer that way. I was taking things slowly with my ex, but then after two months, she confronted me about it. I knew I wanted to be with her, so I made it more serious, but if I hadn't wanted to, I would've fucked around with the answer."

"Yeah, but when I said I couldn't see him anymore, he'd say all this shit to me like he cared," I said.

"Maybe he did to a degree, but it doesn't mean he wants a relationship. It's convenient for some guys just to have you there when they want. So, if you keep going every time he wants it, you make it easy for him. And guys do talk shit... you're right. I think people do in general. But if a guy really wants more with you, he won't try to sleep with you immediately. It won't be his only agenda every time he sees you," he said.

"What's that say about you tonight then?" I asked.

"Don't start that. If I recall correctly, you're the one who asked if I'm gonna kiss you properly and were the one up against that wall. We've both equally been in this tonight."

"Hmmm," I said lightheartedly while making a face at him. "Anyway, what were you saying before that?" I asked.

"What I was saying is that he'll make more of an effort than trying to keep you indoors all the time. And the most important thing, his actions will match his words," he said.

"That makes sense," I answered, reflecting on those guys that it seemed like a chore for them to go on a date. They always wanted to stay in and watch a movie or order food in.

"I think you'll know by his actions what stage a guy is at. We always say people give us mixed messages, but I think we know. We just don't want to face it. I don't even have to tell you this stuff; you know it in your heart. It doesn't matter what else he says or tries to make you believe," he answered.

I'm starting to think I didn't want to ask any more, but it was too tempting.

"And do you know what pisses me off sometimes?" he asked.

"What?"

"When a girl willingly sleeps with me and then blames me if she feels like shit afterward. Why does the guy always get the blame? We're both adults—if we commit to having sex in that moment, we need to take accountability for our own actions," he said passionately.

"I get where she's coming from because she probably likes you, but if she's having sex with you and you never spoke about it being anything more, then that's on her too," I said. "But how can you sleep with so many girls and not feel anything?"

"I don't know. Honestly. I think most guys don't get emotionally attached with sex as often. I mean, we do fall for girls sometimes, but usually we don't feel like we've given anything up if we sleep with someone random," he said.

"So, do guys think I'm a slut if I sleep with them too early when meeting? It plays on my mind if they don't contact me again," I said, remembering that feeling.

"No, it doesn't mean he looks at you as bad or a slut. If he has any maturity, he won't think that. Most guys just won't think too much into it at all. Their silence isn't because they think badly of you; it's because maybe they're only interested in sex. And obviously, I'm generally speaking from being a guy and listening to them speak my whole life. But I'm sure there are exceptions to the rule. This is just what I've experienced and know," he said.

"Fuck, you're honest at least," I said, having mixed emotions. I felt good knowing they don't all think bad of me, but at the same time, it was weird knowing some of the guys I liked didn't feel the same.

"You wanted to know ... and I'm drunk. You've caught me at a good time," he responded. "If we know the girl and have feelings for her, that's a different story. Now I'm not making excuses or even saying it's right, but you told me not to sugarcoat it. I'm being as straight as I can."

"No, I want to know," I said. I knew it would make me overthink it for a while, but randomly approaching this dating game isn't any better. Maybe subconsciously I already knew a lot of what he was saying to be true; I just needed to hear it again to make better decisions.

Nick looked over to me and said, "One of my closest friends called me up once and said that she regretted sleeping with this guy. When I asked why she did it in the first place, she said, 'Because I didn't think he would see me again if I didn't.' To be honest, if that's why you're sleeping with someone, it's probably not worth it. Do you really want to sleep with someone who you think wouldn't see you again if you didn't? Think about it. Guys would probably kill me if they found out I was telling girls not to sleep with them, so I'm sort of breaking a bit of a man code here—"

"Go on," I interrupted.

"Look, I can tell you're a sweet girl. Just be more cautious and take charge of your decisions. You can be in the driver's seat. You can demand respect. If they don't want to see you because you won't sleep with them every time, I doubt that's the guy who will make you happy," he continued, waking me up even more.

"Do they lose interest when I show my vulnerable side? Do they think I'm weak when I care?" I asked.

"Not at all, especially if he has gotten to know you. I know from experience that when I really reflect, I think about the girls who treated me well. You can't help but think about someone who poured out their heart to you. But that doesn't mean he wants a relationship, with you or with anyone. Everyone is searching for different things; you have to accept that."

"You know what I absolutely hate too?" I asked.

"What?"

"I can't stand how some people just change. It's like you're all cool, speak a lot, even become close, and then they just ignore you. Literally out of nowhere, they just don't text back. I could never do that to someone. It's so disgusting," I said.

"It's sickening, I agree. It's like, 'Just tell me if you're seeing someone or don't want to talk anymore,' but to ignore someone you spoke to so often … that's fucked," Nick added.

"Most guys these days don't even want to talk; they literally just want to have sex. If they're upfront and tell me they only want something casual, I might be up for it, but don't lie or lead me on," I said.

"Yeah, I get it," he replied. "I guess some guys just see different girls for different things. I'm sure girls do that with guys too," he continued then stood up.

"What do you mean?" I asked.

"I don't know, Amelia. I think we should just leave the chat here and go downstairs," he said, trying to avoid telling me.

"No. Spit it out … you said you'd be honest," I said, pushing him.

"Why do you fucking want to know all this? Just leave it."

"Because it's not working out there for me, okay? I constantly feel like shit over guys. I need clarity, so I can make better decisions. Now, can you please just help me? They say the truth hurts, but the truth also sets you free. Set me free by helping me make the right choices," I said, tearing up.

The alcohol was definitely getting to my emotions. I internally composed myself before he thought I was some overdramatic weirdo.

He came back over and sat on the bed. "Okay, okay. Chill. Guys have girls for different things based on attraction and connection."

"Yeah, and ... ?" I pushed.

"Some girls they see as a friend but might still want to sleep with them at some point. Girls they can hang out with at home after sex (but won't take them out publicly), and other girls they only want to have a quickie with then leave. Then there are other girls they sleep with who they take out sometimes but don't want to commit. Then, of course, other girls they want to settle down with. And I'm not saying that they do this deliberately ... it's just how they feel about certain people," he said.

Oh my God, what fucking category I am in with some of these guys? I thought, shaking my head and thinking about some of the guys I've been with.

"You wanted to know, Amelia. And don't take it the wrong way. We don't sit there and say, 'This girl is going in that category, this one in that.' We connect with different people differently. I'm sure you don't want to date every guy you hook up with," he said.

"It's a bit hard to swallow," I said.

"Yeah, well, when a great guy does come along, that's when girls have to stop their bullshit and give someone like that a chance. If you keep rejecting guys who are making a real effort to take you out and get to know you, then you're also the problem. Sorry to break it to you. Meet them halfway. If what you're going for now isn't working for you, make changes. You gotta get real as well," he said, looking into my eyes.

Without asking each other, I took the drink from his hand, and he took the cigarette from mine.

"I know you're right. I have to make changes and actually stick to them. I need to change my whole mind-set about this and see people by their actions, not who I want them to be," I replied, taking a deep breath and lying back on the bed. Nick laid down next to me.

"Do you know what?" he asked after we'd been quiet for a few moments.

"What?" I responded.

"So many girls get it wrong. They think the guy who is distant and doesn't show much emotion is strong, that subconsciously he is a 'man.' They are confusing what a real man is. Let me tell you, most of those 'men' are the most scared people I've ever come across. Some of them are the weakest I've ever met. Behind the hard shell, they fear," he said.

"I guess. It's like a lot of girls I know. The ones who are the most closed off, rude, or seem like they are better than everyone else are usually the weakest emotionally," I replied. "Ahh, I don't know...it's just all so confusing out there."

Nick turned his head to me. "No, it's not. It's only as confusing as you make it out to be. It's actually pretty simple when you look at it properly. We just make out like it's complicated because we have been made to believe that what's real is boring. But that's so far from the truth.

"What matters is what's in someone's heart. That should be the first thing we look at after knowing we're attracted. Because if you don't like what's in their heart, nothing else matters. I think many of us have become so distant from our own soul, we ignore people's hearts completely. We stay fixated on their surface qualities or want to control the situation. We have to see beyond that and accept what we're shown about someone's true character. Whether it's positive or negative, we have to make decisions according to that," Nick continued.

"Yeah, you're a hundred percent right. Bit of a deep chat for a Saturday night," I joked.

CHAPTER 18

NOT AS "OPEN"

Nick

After having those conversations with Jordan and Amelia, it's made me more at peace with how I approach my life now and, in a lot of ways, cemented certain views that I have.

I don't buy the belief that being open means I should allow anyone into my sacred space and that, if I don't, it means I am closed off. It's taken a while to build up my mind again, and I don't want it to be at the mercy of just anybody. I'll be honest. I'm not as open with people in the beginning as I used to be; that's not a bad thing. I'm allowed to protect myself from people. And why should I be so open in the beginning? I don't know what their intentions are, what stage they're at in their life, or what they want from me. I believe that trust is built. I don't just trust anyone with my thoughts and emotions, and by having that mind-set, it prevents me from not getting overly emotional with everyone I meet.

I acknowledge that people might not be who I assume they are or who they claim to be when first meeting them. There is liberation in understanding that. It's not being pessimistic; it's being realistic. People might say that mind-set is negative, that not being open restricts me from finding happiness, but I don't live my life waiting for someone else to complete me. I'm not selfish enough to have someone in my life only for that reason. If I have a partner in my life, it's because I want them, not because I feel like I need them to live. I think that's more special. To know you're with someone by your free, thoughtful choice rather than driven by your insecurities.

There was a time when I invested all I had in someone. I loved everything about her. I loved the shape of her body. I loved her small hands against mine, the way her lips moved when she spoke, how her eyebrows scrunched when she was angry, the way she smelled, the way she held me. Any imperfections she had, I loved them too. I never took advantage of her vulnerability or wanted her to feel insecure with me. I did everything I could to ease her pain, to support her, to care for her. But in the end, no matter how much I did for her, it wasn't enough.

I assumed that the character of the girl I met was who she was going to be forever. I ignored my underlying wisdom, which says that people can change. During the relationship, I felt like she changed drastically. However, looking back, maybe she was trying to be someone she wasn't just to keep me around. Maybe she was always the person I was awakened to in the end. She completely broke my heart that day she said she didn't want to be with me anymore. And maybe, in some respect, I'm still putting it back together.

So really, who did I give myself to? The person she claimed to be when I first met her, that's who. I took what she showed me at face value and swallowed it whole. But eventually, the truth revealed itself to me, and it wasn't pretty. I didn't want to accept the person I had gotten to know was gone; that she was someone else. I kept giving "my all" to her in the hope that I could revive the beautiful person who died a long time before. I should've accepted it and started making arrangements to move on. But just like the death of anyone you care about, you don't want to let go. You don't want to face reality, so you hold on, hoping they'll return, hoping that you can regain that feeling of having them around.

A client of mine who is in her sixties and has been married for more than forty years said to me in front of her husband, "You never know anyone fully, no matter if you've been with them for a whole lifetime. We are always learning about each other. You both have to be open to that. It's the only way you can adapt for so long." I didn't want to believe that at the time because I was deeply in love with my girlfriend and thought I knew all of her. I'd thought we had the fairy-tale relationship. I was even thinking of proposing when we had only been together for six months. Only a few short months later, I was forced to comprehend a lot of what that client said to me. It taught me a lot, made me more aware. It made me look beyond the surface.

I now understand that, when someone rejects me, it's not always a reflection of me. Timing is a big factor when meeting someone. I always say timing and circumstance are underrated. Who knows what they've been through recently? I'm not in the same headspace every time I catch up with someone. All things, good or bad, can affect my demeanor, which then depicts what vibe I give off. And this new person will most likely judge my whole character on that. But there's so much more to me. It's timing, it's where someone's at, it's how open or closed they are, and it's how ready they feel. Humans have many different layers; we are complex beings.

I don't really know why I became cold toward those who treated me well and chased those who played hard to get; it's just who I was. It's like when we meet someone, there's subconscious pressure for it to be something or not. We're always anxious over our love lives. And if it doesn't exactly sync in that moment...next. That pressure doesn't always serve the cause. Maybe it's because our souls thrive for a real connection and for real love in a world that is so virtual. We want real, but we're appreciating it much less.

Maybe the question isn't "What do we all really want as a generation?" Maybe it's "What do I really want as an individual?" Then I have to find someone who wants the same things and stop trying to force someone who I know doesn't. We all want vastly different things for our life, which to me is great, because we live in a world that can make that possible. But it means we have to find that person who is on the same page. In saying that, I guess a lot of people aren't ready for a relationship, even when they think they want it.

One of the grayest areas in the modern dating world is that so many people think they want a relationship but don't want to face the realities that come along with it. We can't handle them when we do commit, and in addition to that, most people don't even understand what commitment means anymore. In a relationship, half our thinking and decisions becomes someone else's. We have to think of how it will affect them, not just ourselves. Nearly everything we do is influenced to a degree, even if just by their presence. You're no longer allowed to be as selfish as you are when you're single. It's a team effort. I also believe that there has to be a great level of respect. Someone can love you and still do things to disrespect you. But when someone truly respects you, they won't do things that they know will hurt you.

People get into relationships not facing these realities first. That's why I'm not in one at the moment. Right now, I don't want those responsibilities. Sure, it crosses my mind to spend my life with someone special and have kids one day, but I want to make sure I'm really ready, and I want to make sure the other person understands it too. I don't want to live my life wanting to believe someone will understand it in time. No, the next woman I want to be with has to understand what forever means. Because that's the commitment I make when I get into a relationship. Sure, there are no guarantees in life, but I'm past that stage of just committing ignorantly.

I've heard some people say, "You'll know instantly when you meet the person you're going to spend the rest of your life with." I think that was more relatable when the old concept of settling down was engrained in society. Our parents' and grandparents' eras were vastly different from ours, but we still want to hold on to that concept of a relationship. I'm not saying it doesn't work anymore. I'm just saying it's becoming less frequent. And I think it's because admiring what was back then, while wanting what is today, contradict each other in a lot of ways. We live in a vastly different world. The older generations were taught different things and had different priorities. They had a different upbringing.

I think, to a large degree, we look back and think they met and fell in love ignorantly. I disagree. I think they were very certain about what they wanted. And when they met it, they didn't overthink it as much. They pursued it. Maybe we have made things so complicated that being certain again is actually the simplest way of finding and accepting love. Now, I think too many options weigh on our mind. There's more to it. I think a lot of it has to do with ourselves and where we're at, emotionally and mentally. I think most people in our generation assume that the grass is always greener on the other side…until it isn't. It's like we're never content. And a lot of times, we find ourselves searching for something we've already had. That's why our decisions must be made carefully.

We live in a fast-moving world now, a higher-stimulating one. People are taught that freedom and independence are a greater solution for fulfillment. That remains in the back of our minds and surfaces when things aren't running smoothly in our relationships with others. So often, people don't look at how a relationship will add to their life but rather what it's going to take away. This is the generation where we do what we want, when we want to do it. We hate having our actions questioned, and we definitely don't want to feel like we're living in someone else's shadow. But I think we still look at the older generations as a basis to judge our relationships, not because we want it to go back to the way it was, but because we still believe in a "forever love." Because we still find substance in the values they upheld with each other. And we're trying to come to terms with how to apply those values in the generation we're now in. We're trying to understand how much it all means to us. I think we have to accept each other's individual lifestyles now, stop thinking we own this person, and be freer in our love for them. That, to me, is love in the twenty-first century. To let each other be what they want and to make sure they can both accept that before making the commitment. Until we accept the freedom of new while committing to those fundamental values of old—such as respect, support, selflessness at times, and loyalty—most will still be very lost.

CHAPTER 19

UBER RIDE HOME

Amelia

I called Zara's phone from the other room because I didn't want to interrupt anything.

"Hey," Zara answered quietly.

"Hey, I'm just downstairs. Do you want to leave?" I said.

"Yeah. Give me a second. Jordan fell asleep," she whispered.

A few minutes later, Zara walked downstairs, looking a little worse for wear.

"Thanks for everything," Zara said to Nick.

"Yeah, thanks. I really appreciate it," I added.

Nick looked pretty tired too. "No problem. Are you sure you don't want me to order you an Uber?" he asked.

"No, thanks. We already got one. I think it's nearly here, so we'd better head downstairs," I answered.

I grabbed my bag and kissed Nick good-bye.

We got in the backseat of the Uber and started heading back to our hotel.

"You guys were so loud... me and Nick could hear you from downstairs," I said to Zara.

"His dick was perfect. He felt amazing," Zara replied.

"I could hear him slapping your ass. He didn't seem like the rough type, though."

"Sometimes it's the ones you least expect. And Oh my God, he was whispering in my ear when he was bending me over. Saying stuff like, "You're my girl now," and then slapping it. Then he said, "I don't want anyone else inside you. Do you understand?" And pulled my hair back even harder until I said yes.

"It's weird... sometimes sex talk can turn me off, but it's like he claimed me. It made me more into it. He knew the balance," she said. "We literally both came at the same time. ... Fuck, he was good. Oops, sorry about this," Zara added to the sixty-something-year-old female driver.

"I'm trying to ignore most of it," she said, raising her eyebrows and looking a little disgusted.

"He made you come? You haven't come with a guy in forever," I whispered so the driver couldn't hear us.

"Yes, with his dick, too, not even his fingers. I did not expect that from him. Oh, and his tongue was heaven. That guy knows what he's doing. I hope he texts me. Anyway, what happened with you and Nick?" Zara asked.

"Nothing. Well, he went down on me for a bit, and it felt amazing, but then I saw a camera and freaked out."

"A camera? What the fuck?"

"Don't worry. It was off. I don't really want to think about it again. I embarrassed myself. But we ended up having a really good chat. Some of the things he said really woke me up," I answered. "I think I'm gonna cut the trip short, babe. I might leave tomorrow instead. I just feel like I've gotten what I want from it. It's time to go back home and face everything properly. I need to change a few things and get on with my life," I said.

"Are you sure?" Zara asked.

"Yeah…it's time," I answered, taking a deep breath.

August 21, 2019, at 12:10 a.m.

It's like guys have it too easy these days.they don't have to take us out for dinner or anything. We just sleep with them without them making any real effort.

i want to be respected too, then I'll be more wild for him than he ever imagined.

If I can love the wrong person this much, think of how much I could love the right one

I know I haven't made all the right decisions,but some have been just straightout ignorant. Especially when I continued to give myself to someone who took me for a ride. It's like being the passenger in a car going sixty miles an hour straight into a wall.you're too busy trying to talk sense into the driver, you forget to save yourself from crashing

a relationship isn't about one person trying to force a connection. If it's not reciprocated, move on.

August 28, 2019, at 3:35 p.m.

If they're making you feel down more than making you feel great, then there's your answer

I want to start focusing more of my energy toward loving myself, rather than on the way others treat me. I want to start waking up everyday again smiling and looking forward to the day, free from any bad emotional attachment.i don't want my mood to change so quickly.

No one is going to stop me from shining no matter how badly they treat me. No one is going to stop me living the best possible life I can live. I'll pick myself up, I'll work it out, and I'll keep going.

I know what it's like to be with someone who brought out the worst emotions in me. Never again…

•••

OPEN DELTA

One year passed…

MERKABA

Two years passed...

CHAPTER 20

THREE YEARS LATER

Well, the past few years definitely had their ups and downs. I've had some of the most amazing times of my life and, of course, some challenges. I met a lot of guys within that time too, and my experience with Jay did affect it. They say getting your heart broken is similar to grieving a death. I have experienced deaths, and it honestly wasn't as bad as being rejected by the only person I thought I wanted love from. Most people who have died didn't have a choice. You learn to reason with that. But to have someone you gave your heart to say, more or less, "I can be with you, but I don't want to be," is like seeing the person you thought was dead living another life and being happier because you're not in it. That abandonment was the worst feeling I have felt. It was hell.

For a long time, I was really unsettled. I had to face a lot of my demons and come to terms with what I deserved. I wanted to be stronger and more aware the next time I dated someone. I referred to so many guys I met as being narcissistic, and maybe that was true, but what I neglected was that I was actually being narcissistic to my own soul. Being closed off to it, pretending to be someone I'm not, manipulating it to accept things it didn't deserve, always making excuses to it. And all my soul wanted that whole time was to be true to myself. When I met someone I was really into, I expected it not to work out. My mind automatically thought of what could go wrong, and my insecurities forced me to believe they would lose interest in me. Every time I kissed them good-bye, I felt like they could be gone forever. Even if a guy really liked me, it was my disbelief that someone I wanted could be that genuine. And the more I feared losing someone, the less control I had over the situation, the less control I had over myself. I realize now that I wasn't looking *for* love; I was anxiously looking to *be* loved. I valued my self-worth on the attention others were willing to give me. That's why I always got hurt. That's why I always doubted myself.

I needed to have that awareness of what I truly wanted in someone. That needed to be louder than any situation I found myself in. I was never to forget what my experiences taught me; it was the only way I was going to make right decisions for my life. I started noticing certain qualities in people, and ones similar to Jay were a lot more obvious. Looking back, it's hard to see why I wanted people like Jay in my life. It's hard to see why I allowed myself to get into things like petty social media games. I don't think I truly loved them for who they were but loved the idea of what I thought it could be. It was all a delusion. I now understand that many of my past feelings disguised themselves as love, but those masks fell off. They made me believe that love is something it isn't.

Love is beautiful, not always energy-draining. Love is understanding, even in times of hardship. Love is compromising. Love goes both ways. Love is hard but should be equally rewarding. Love takes time. And yeah, love is the scariest thing in the world sometimes, but when it's real, you find the courage to be who you want and say what you want to that person. It's more comfortable. It's not so closed off. After my breakup, I wondered whether I'd ever love my future partner (whoever that was going to be) as much as the person who broke my heart. But then I realized that people like Jay were only willing to give me the parts of them they wanted to give, when they wanted to give them. The good parts they were willing to share always had an expiration date. That's not love. Once the dust had settled from my last breakup, I couldn't really see a future with him even if he did want to come back. I've also learned that some of those guys who rejected me never thought they were "better" than I was. I never lost anything. That was only in my head. Most times, they weren't thinking about it at all. They just had their own set of values, their own wants, and their own problems. We're all different; I had to accept that.

I stopped ignoring things about people just because I was attracted to them. I learned to follow my initial gut feeling. The connection meant more to me. How I truly felt about them, not just what I saw, who they were, not what they were, was the new bar I set. What also helped me feel freer was admitting that I really didn't want a relationship when I wasn't ready. I felt like a weight had been lifted off my shoulders. When I still found myself being too caught up on people I didn't know very well, I knew it wasn't time. I had to be honest with myself and say that I'm not ready instead of wanting to believe I was. I wasn't wise enough or strong enough within myself yet. I didn't want to put all of myself into another person, not again, not so soon. It gave me time and space to reflect on my experiences and create new ones. I wanted to live.

I even made little changes, which had a big impact on helping me re-center myself. I started checking my phone on my terms. I turned off vibrate when it was on silent. I wanted "me" time, and I noticed that the buzzing removed me from that. If I was waiting for an important call, I put it on loud, but mostly throughout my day, silent meant silent. If people got upset at me for not responding to them instantly, that was their problem. It was so invigorating. Fuck, those messages and notifications could change my mood so easily. And it wasn't even the things I was seeing but the things I wasn't.

Checking to see if someone had texted me back and realizing they hadn't also changed my mood. It was an addiction. And just like any addiction, it wasn't good for my mental health. Admittedly, the smallest, dumbest things still get to me sometimes. I'm not bulletproof; nobody is. But when that's happening too often, I know it's time to start reconnecting with my soul again. In fact, it reminds me that I need to connect with it every day.

I've stopped wanting to live my whole life comparing myself to other people or filling my thoughts with garbage. I really need my time alone, away from everything; then I feel I can deal with the world and enjoy it more in peace, with more inner strength. I think I'm equally an introvert and an extrovert, if that exists. And I've noticed that, when I get back to my essence, I lose the desire to want to control everything outside, and that makes me a lot less anxious. I finally feel like I'm living life through my soul again, rather than just through my head. Now I focus more on my goals and experience things in the real world. Yeah, I still have Insta and other apps, but I'm not on them as much. And if I do find myself getting too wrapped up into them again, I limit it. I'm more aware of the impact it can have on my life. I spend more of my time with people who actually mean something to me and stop trying to impress people I probably don't even like. I've started learning to be me again. I even took up acting classes two nights a week and sometimes rock climbing on weekends. I'm trying new things, and they're unlocking creativity and power that I never knew I had.

I also traveled more than I ever have and explored more sexually within the past three years. I definitely went through a wild stage (or a wild stage for me, anyway). I learned a lot about who I was. Some things that I did I wasn't overly proud of and felt a bit weird afterward, but others helped me find what I really wanted. About two years ago, I had a sexual experience that had only ever crossed my mind, something I never thought I'd actually commit to. I had my first threesome. One day, it came up in a drunken conversation on Friday after-work drinks with a married female colleague. Her partner came down and joined us at the bar and we got even more drunk. I had to get drunk. I was ridiculously nervous. He was handsome and had this relaxed energy that made me more comfortable. I never felt pressured. We eventually got into a taxi and went back to their place.

I must admit, for a while after that, I was hornier than I'd ever been. It even made me question the concept of monogamy. It just unlocked a part of me that I never knew existed, although I still contained it. I only ever had one threesome after that, about six months later. But this time, it was with two guys on my holiday in Bali. I just packed up and went for a whole month on my own. I was at a stage where I had to be somewhere other than home. My mind needed new stimulation to get away from the repetitiveness of Western working society. Catching the same train, walking the same streets, seeing the same faces, having the same conversations... it all got too much.

I met these two guys at the beginning of my trip who were best friends. They really took me in; I felt like I'd known them forever. We hung out for about a week, and then one night, we were all at a party, but the place was really hot inside, and people were getting ridiculously drunk. One of the guys suggested that we go back to their villa and hop in the private pool. We ended up skinny-dipping. I felt so free when I was swimming naked. I'd been eating so much in Bali too, I felt like my body wasn't up to shape, but I didn't care. There was something about that vacation that just washed away a lot of my insecurities.

One thing soon led to another. We started kissing and touching each other in the pool. Not long after, we went into the shower and started having sex, and then the bedroom. It was the most erotic experience I've ever had. I wasn't as nervous as I was with the couple. This time, I completely surrendered myself to their masculine energy. I loved the way they both took control... they didn't just fuck me but made love to me as well. It was like all three of us were one for that moment, so comfortable with each other. I lost the feeling of being judged... I just let go. Around that period, I also went through a stage where I was more drawn to older men. I liked their energy; I needed it at that time. In the end, though, none of that really fulfilled me. Definitely no regrets; I did what I did and enjoyed it at the time, but it's not the life I wanted to live consistently. The great thing about experience is that it teaches you what you really want.

CHAPTER 21

THE BEGINNING

After my New York vacation with Zara, I kept in touch with Nick. We became really close, almost like best friends. At one point, we spoke every day through WhatsApp. I had never spoken to a guy so much, not even guys I had dated. He was in London, but he felt so present... it was weird. I was still in shock that he was even remotely interested in me. I felt like he was way out of my league, but maybe that was my self-doubt still rearing its ugly head. After his trip to London, he came to San Fran for a month for work. We spent a lot of time together. Lunch dates would lead into dinner, which then always seemed to lead into drinks. I would often catch myself looking at him when he was distracted with what to order. He does this cute little frown between his brows when he's concentrating and is always so polite to the staff. I also noticed how much he laughed at my somewhat pathetic jokes. I'm someone who tends to laugh at my own jokes a lot, but he genuinely seemed to like them. He had this way of making me feel comfortable being myself but still get butterflies every time I saw him.

We also spoke way too much while cuddling up on the couch watching Netflix. We would have to replay half the episodes because we literally couldn't keep quiet. Hearing him talk about his family made me get this fulfilling feeling in my heart. I could tell how much he adored them by the way his energy lit up every time they were mentioned. I couldn't help but think about what he would be like as a husband or even a dad. I felt so connected with him, not just sexually, but mentally and spiritually too. I felt like we had known each other forever, but to be honest, I didn't know if he was looking into it as much as I was.

At that time—which was about two and half years ago—I didn't know what Nick's true intentions were between us. He never brought it up and neither did I. We both just went along with it. I think a small part of me was scared to ask if it meant more to him in case I got rejected but mainly because I knew I wasn't ready either. He ended up basing himself back in New York but still traveled a lot. It was too risky for me to keep in touch with him as often as I was, so I decided to slow down contact. We still video called here and there but not as much. I didn't want to get even more emotionally involved when I didn't know where in the world he would be next. I didn't want that uncertainty again with someone I really liked. And back then, there was still so much I had to learn. I was still dealing with a lot of pain from my ex.

The last time I saw him was about three months ago. He was in San Fran again but this time only for four nights. We hung out and kissed but didn't sleep together. I wasn't willing to sleep with him again and then not see him for a while. We spoke about some of our experiences and even people we had dated. I must say, I think there was a bit of jealousy hearing it on both on our ends. I also told him about my vacation to Thailand that I've planned.

Seeing Nick again not too long ago, I noticed my feelings toward him were still raw. He helped me grow so much, especially from that chat we had in New York. That basically sent me on a new journey. Our contact started picking up again after I saw him last, although for the past two weeks, I hadn't heard from him until he messaged me the other day. What he said completely took me by surprise.

He sent me this long text:

Dear Amelia,

The other day when I was driving, I had this overwhelming feeling to tell you something, but I didn't. I got on with my week until today came. And to be honest, I'm sick of holding myself back. I know this might seem like it's coming out of nowhere, but it's been playing on my mind for a long time. So here I go…

The feelings I have for you are so deep. I think much deeper than you've ever known. Sometimes, even when I'm halfway across the world, I think about the way I feel when I'm around you or when I see your smile over our video chats. It makes me smile no matter where I am. Last week, I was re-watching that video you sent me of your little cousins

jumping on you, and I just started randomly
smiling. I didn't realize it, but I must have
been looking at this old woman while doing
it. This is no joke…she actually smiled
back and kissed the air looking straight
at me. I didn't know what to do haha

But seriously, your energy, I don't know…I'm
just so drawn to it. Sometimes I try to push
away the thought because I think it's easier,
but then I just miss your presence. I miss your
laugh. I miss your warmth. And the small,
weird things you do. I miss them all. There
are things about you that make me see how
special you are. I've had a lot of time to think
since we last met, and there are some things
I'd really like to say to you and ask in person.

I don't know if you'd be up for this, but I'd
love to meet you in Thailand when you're
there and talk properly. I'm going to be
in Singapore for work, but I can come
over. I understand if you don't want to.

Nick :)

I was taking Scruffy for a walk around the park when I got it and had to stop and sit down. My heart melted reading it. I started crying. And the fact that he started it with "Dear Amelia" made it just that little bit cuter. Excitement and happiness came over me, but then later in the night, caution. I questioned whether it was fear, and if so, if a bit of fear was even a bad thing. I think I became cautious because I don't want people to think they can come into my life whenever they feel like it. I need to know he's for real.

I would definitely pursue something with Nick, and that's not just because of his looks. I mean, I'm definitely one of those people who need to be really attracted to someone to be with them. But in saying that, I don't always think being attracted to someone and them being "great looking" are always related. At first sight, I can be really drawn by someone's looks, but that's not enough to keep me attracted to them. Sometimes I've been more attracted to people who aren't anywhere near as good- looking as some others I've met. It's the unexplainable things that draw me in. I connect with Nick too, but if I didn't know he's a great guy and have the morals and values

I look for, I wouldn't even bother. I couldn't live my life with someone just because of their looks or their career. Maybe some girls can, but it's not me.

The truth is, I'm in a really good place in my life at the moment and don't need anyone. I don't want it to be about needing anyone. I want it to be about wanting them. I don't want to feel like I need anyone to live my life ever again. I would love Nick to be a part of it, but unless I know he's serious, I refuse to get involved in the whole casual "see how things go" terms. I'm not just "going with the flow" anymore when it comes to my love life. It needs to be more obvious. I'm done with having to keep guessing. His words won't show me how serious he is, as beautiful as they are. It's his actions that will, and that's why I've decided to meet him in Thailand and see what he's going to suggest. To be honest, a part of me also wants to know what these "weird little things" are that I do and why he is so drawn to me. I am nervous because it's coming up next month and could potentially be the start of something new. It's still going to be a risk putting myself out there again, but a calculated risk this time filled with a lot more experience and wisdom. I'm stronger now.

I remember there was one morning about a year ago when something dawned on me. As I was putting on my clothes in front of the mirror, I stopped, stared at myself, and thought, *You're fucking tough.* It was like someone slapped me in the face and woke me up. I've been through so much shit and I survived. I've gotten through everything life has thrown me and am still here standing. I had this sudden appreciation for myself. I now know that, without self-love, nothing else matters. Meditation really helps me attain love for myself. It clears out all the garbage from my mind. And you know, I could hate people who have hurt me in the past; that's easy, but to wish them well is my true self. I think it shows a lot about someone's character when they can still be nice to others after being hurt so deeply. In the end, not letting someone turn me sour toward life is where my true power lies. I want to live on a higher vibration.

I often hear people say, "Life is something that you just can't work out." And I guess to some degree, I was someone who was always confused about most things in my life. But when I think about it, I've actually worked out a lot. I've worked out that I don't know everything, that I'm still learning every day, and that's okay. I've worked out that I'm not proud of some of the things I've done in my life, but other things I am. I've worked out that I'm not always going be happy, that sometimes I'm still scared about what my future holds, that I'm not bulletproof. I've worked out that sometimes I can't control how some people treat me, but in the end, I can control how much I let it affect me. I've worked out that love feels better than hate, that I should embrace those who love me, not the memory of those who pretended to love me. I've worked out that I want to give my time to people who help lift me up, not always make me doubt myself. I've worked out that I shouldn't hate the scars on my heart but be proud of what they've taught me. I've worked out that, no matter how hard life is sometimes, it doesn't make it any less beautiful, in fact, sometimes even more so. I've worked out how important my choices are in shaping my life.

I now know that a lot of the way I felt was because of my decisions, and more times than not, I do my best to make better ones. That higher level of consciousness has really given me a sense of control again. I could have continued using the same line, "That was meant to be," or base my life's events on some destiny, but I know one thing: it's my decisions that have equally shaped my life, for good or bad. And I need to make those decisions with what I've worked out in my life so far. From this day forward, my freedom lies in knowing I have choices in my life, and I'm the one who makes them. My life is mine; it's what I choose for it, it's who I choose to have a part of it. And knowing I have that power over my life makes me smile. I feel freer. I feel alive again.

Amelia Golding

LOTUS

Her eyes opened slowly and then closed again. As she took another glimpse, fear suddenly took over. She thought she was in a place that was unfamiliar to her. Her body froze; her mind raced.

She was lying on a dirt path a few feet wide and wearing a black dress. There were two high walls on either side of her that went as far as she could see. They were made of thick, green plants. Nothing was visible through them. For all she knew, they blocked her in. The sky was clear, the sun shining. She quickly stood up and walked around in a daze.

Where am I?

Frantically trying to find a way out, she couldn't find an exit. She ran and ran and ran, as fast as she could. As she got to the end of the path, she noticed similar paths to her left and right. She turned left. Getting to the end of that path, something dawned on her ... she had been here before. She was in the maze.

It wasn't exactly how she remembered it. She tried to remember how she got out last time, but her memory failed her.

"Hello! Is anyone here?" she yelled repeatedly. Not knowing exactly what her future held, she started to panic.

She quickly composed herself and saw what seemed to be a figure at the end of yet another path. She paced toward it. She finally arrived and saw who it was ... everything inside her told her to run away from him. She did. Looking back to see if danger was following her, she smashed into something and fell on the ground. Everything went blank.

She slowly stood up and noticed that it was a gigantic mirror as wide as the path that had stopped her in her tracks. There was no getting past it. She had to face it. A quote soon appeared on the glass:

Sometimes in life, there is no way out,
but there is always a way through.

The sun's rays landed on the thick, green plant wall. She walked over and managed to push her way through. As she got to the other side, she looked down at her hand and noticed old scars on her knuckles. She grinned.

"I know Amelia has been telling a lot of people about what happened in our relationship, but there are always two sides to every story. She wasn't perfect either, you know."

Jay

@TheModernBreakUpBook
@Daniel_Chidiac

www.themodernbreakup.com
www.undercoverpubhouse.com

CPSIA information can be obtained
at www.ICGtesting.com
Printed in the USA
BVHW070714160620
581552BV00004B/354

9 780987 166555